The Dream Life of Larry Rios

A novel

Alex Z. Salinas

FlowerSong Press
Copyright © 2025 by Alex Z. Salinas

ISBN: 978-1-963245-68-4

Published by FlowerSong Press
in the United States of America.
www.flowersongpress.com

Cover Art and Illustrations Credit: Lisa Oakes
Cover Design Credit: Daniel Paniagua
Cover Layout & Design Credit: Carlos Fidel Espinoza
Typesetting: Carlos Fidel Espinoza
Set in Adobe Garamond Pro

NOTICE: SCHOOLS AND BUSINESSES
FlowerSong Press offers copies of this book at quantity discount with
bulk purchase for educational, business, or sales promotional use.

For information, please email the Publisher
at info@flowersongpress.com.

Edward Vidaurre
Publisher/Editor-in-chief
FlowerSong Press
www.flowersongpress.com

For Mom and Dad, bibliophiles and bibliomaniacs, broken clocks & Beauty.

It was strange to have no self—to be like a little boy left alone in a big house, who knew that now he could do anything he wanted to do, but found that there was nothing that he wanted to do—

-F. Scott Fitzgerald

And it's also not unusual that if you're a novelist, you're an idiot.

-Valeria Luiselli

Y'all don't want to hear me, you just want to dance

-André 3000

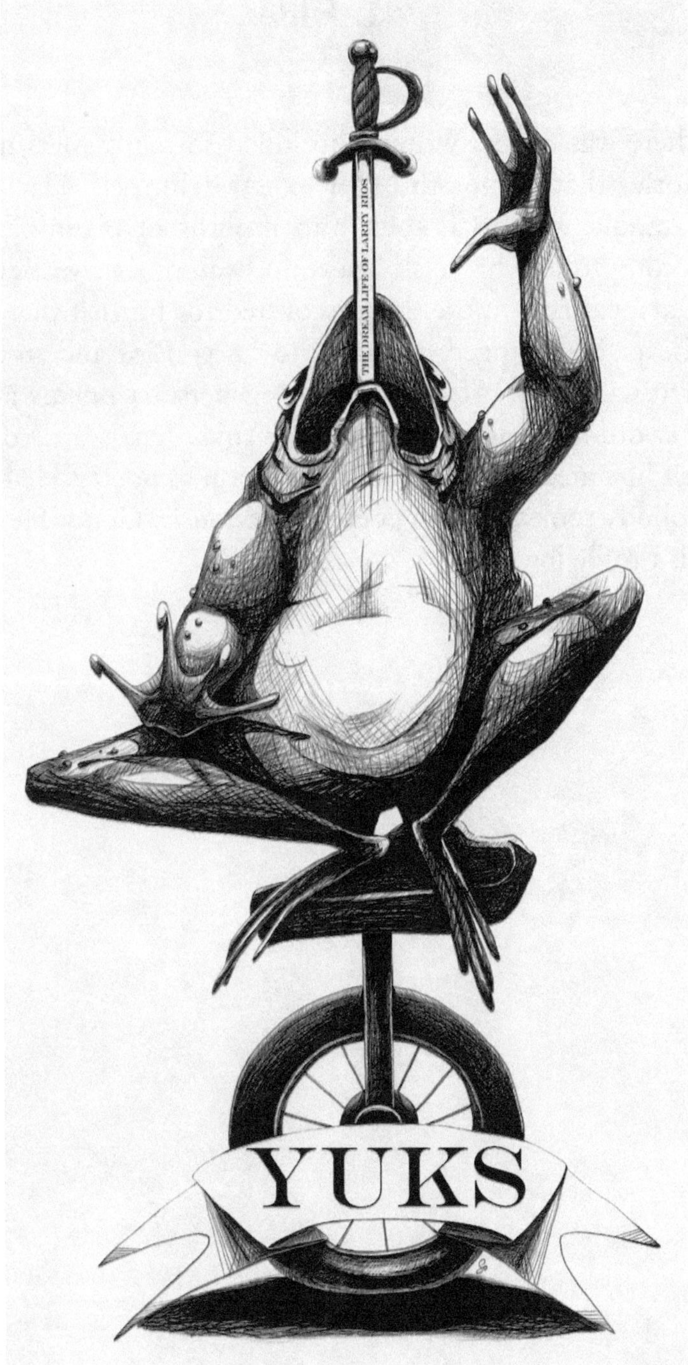

THE DREAM LIFE OF LARRY RIOS
YUKS

1. Hide

There was once a writer who killed so many folks in his stories that he got the idea to try it himself. He was a paranoid type so it took him months of planning. He accomplished his task; cleanup was a doozy. Beyond that I can't say more. He discovered for himself that life's cheap. He changed his name to Larry Rios and stopped writing fiction. He began writing persona poems about a sword-swallowing frog named Yuks. Larry, a divorcee, felt liberated about his transformation to poetry. He knew nobody took Chicano poets too seriously. Good. He kept his profile low.

2. And Seek

Larry Rios, a murderer, hates folks, therefore he writes poetry. He'd read Wittgenstein and Proust, hoping to get tangled between spacetime, but this was back when he penned fiction. No, Larry reminded himself, you're an autodidactic philosopher; no one'll ever read your stuff. Plus, you're a Chicano poet now. Keep a low profile! Larry reveled in his skin—brown with a tint of red. His muddy green eyes won him a wife once but the pandemonium in his brain ruined everything. "Life's cheap," proclaims Larry in the morning. Therefore, poems about sword-swallowing frogs. *Ribbit*! Larry chuckles, his refined sense of humor.

3. Working

Larry Rios writes poetry all day long. Larry Rios has never traveled to Hong Kong. Larry Rios thinks folks are all the same. Larry Rios sets atrocious literature aflame. He'd quit smoking till recently. He'd changed his name for protection. He suffers from existence like everyone. He works an eight-to-five like everyone. He identifies as a Chicano poet. Therefore, he operates on the margins of invention. He created Yuks the sword-swallowing frog; Yuks is blissfully depressed. Larry's poems are obviously metaphorical. Obviously literal. Larry prefers that nobody reads them. He writes all day long. He's always working. He can't say why.

4. Striving

Larry Rios—murderer and unrenowned biodegradable poet—strives to pen the realest poem of all time. How to accomplish that? First, accept that 70% of life is false advertising. Second, appreciate the blood-soaked earth. Third, limit cheesy sentimental adverbs. I mean, really limit them. Last, write opposite of what you'd tell your mother. Easy. Then suddenly Larry is sidetracked at work. He commiserates with colleagues. He reluctantly buys a fish. He thinks about his (s)ex. He chews on last words of his favorite novels. He writes frog poems to generate better ideas. He takes hot showers, hopes the fog inside clears.

5. Insignificance

Nobody taught Larry Rios how to write poems. He learned the old-fashioned way: libraries and doing it yourself. Also, Google. His sanity dissolved upon taking the craft seriously. What an egotistic endeavor, transforming life's surprises into little words nobody asked for, nobody reads, let alone the work of an unrenowned recyclable poet. Larry should've listened to Lucia, his ex; he should've done a whole lot of things. But Larry, he's as stubborn as a grizzled mule. A rebel raconteur who once murdered somebody because death on paper wasn't enough. Larry learned that life's cheap. That we breathe in oxygen—exhale insignificance.

6. Ruined

Jesus. Wittgenstein. Spinoza. Iago. Gene Wilder's Willy Wonka. Larry Rios' favorite philosophers. Larry heard on the radio OMC's "How Bizarre," thought bizarrely of Frantz Fanon. Revolutionaries strike an uncomfortable, familiar nerve in Larry. (Because revolution resides in each of our hearts.) Larry had a home once. Still does, on a different street. Different wavelength. Poetry's ruined Larry, his conscience shot 90% of the time. He's seldom complacent. Some women find this attractive, but that's because Larry doesn't dress like Willy Wonka; he prefers Levi's blue jeans, white Converse Chuck Taylors. Larry, no influencer; a knockoff. "I am what I am not."

7. Huddle

Interiorly, Larry Rios sometimes talks to dead writers. "I suppose you think it's time," he says to James Baldwin, who's nesting a cigarette betwixt his leaden fingers, "that I started acting like a new man?" Baldwin takes a dramatic drag. "Matters not what *I* think, baby, it matters what *you* think." "Tell me about transformation, Jimmy. Tell me how." Another puff, then, "Lots of these," waving his cigarette, then, "And lots of these," grabbing his junk. "Oh snap!" Wary Larry washes his hands (elated afresh to write) in the men's room, thinks, A mystery bag, a beacon of audacity, that guy.

8. The Name

So why the name Larry Rios? For starters, Larry from the Three Stooges was his favorite: clownish curls (like little question marks), ugliest, fictive kin to the other brothers. "Larry" belied false alternatives: Lawrence, Laurel, Lazarus. "Just Larry," a polite recalibration. An undisputed American urge. Meanwhile, Rios rivaled the exotica of Larry's muddy green eyes. Buried jade. Rivers Amazon and Styx flowing into the ocean. Saying what they have to say and evaporating. In this recount, the name Larry Rios can do *anything*. He accepts that life is complications. If only he can become more than a cheerleader for the dead.

9. Irritable

Larry Rios increasingly believes that poets—hotshots and no-names (the invisible majority)—are self-righteous, self-serving and, iconoclastically, mean. If he had to go back and do it all over, he'd probably (positively) still let poetry choose him. An irritating acknowledgement. Okay, maybe some poets are decently centered. Maybe some do hemorrhage generosity. Maybe some're worth their weight in gold, oil, blood. Redeemable. Larry has his bad days, too, like everyone else. Larry gets inexplicably irritable, too, like everyone around. Larry judges books by their covers, too, like everyone ought to. Larry oftentimes needs lovin', too, just like—you guessed it—you.

10. Breathless

One of the worst pieces of writing advice Larry Rios ever received was from a United States Poet Laureate who'd suggested to him to "Get rid of that punctuation" and to Larry this was bewildering because immediately his mind whipped up a frenzy of run-on sentences and then somewhere in the psychic tumult he thought of his poor little creation Yuks the sword-swallowing frog who also seemed disturbed by the proclamation because Yuks unleashed an anxious flurry of *ribbits* and Larry sped home so he could hop in the shower and rinse off the day's contaminants and reset his ruffled worldview.

11. Shoegazing

All he remembers is he was at a café when he first heard Beach House's "Somewhere Tonight." He pulled out his phone and Shazam'd it. At home he downloaded the song and discovered it belonged to a musical subgenre called shoegaze. What a peculiar name, thought Larry Rios. Shoegaze. Like a lullaby the song reminded him of the bayfront, his mother. It made him think of smooth skin, floating castles. He recalled dancing slowly with his ex on their wedding night. Suddenly Larry found himself dancing alone in his living room. Waltzing with a ghost. Gazing down at his feet. Shoegazing.

12. Dreams

Larry Rios is under the impression that repeating one's dreams is like telling someone a joke starting in the middle. "Context is queen," Larry says to his reflection, shaving stubble off his neck, ever so unguarded. Without it, who's to say the president isn't a burning dumpster? That poetry isn't the steamroller of humankind? That Buddha isn't Jesus reincarnated with an appetite? (*Paunch*ius Pilate, anyone?) That the American Dream didn't perish with Amerigo Vespucci? Larry Rios—an only child—doesn't discuss his dreams, insoluble like pi. He's liable to say that the here and now's all we've got. Or something melodramatic.

13. Möbius Strip

Thanks to Jorge Luis Borges' short story, "The Disk," Larry Rios is obsessed with the psychogenic possibility of one-sided objects. This manifests in the form of countless questions: Perhaps wind is one-sided? Perhaps the color red is one-sided? Perhaps the jazz of Coltrane is one-sided? Perhaps the blood of Christ was one-sided? Perhaps the genius of Dalí was one-sided? Perhaps Santa Anna's phantom leg was one-sided? Larry discovers on Google (where else?) loads about the Möbius strip, a mathematically one-sided band—half-twisted paper representing non-Euclidean infinite space. A toy a toddler can assemble. "It is what it isn't," a stupefied utterance.

14. Love

Let us not forget: Larry Rios is a murderer. But listen, if you've never been obsessed, you cannot understand murder. If you've never obtained madness—even in passing—you cannot understand murder. If you've never bled for your stake, you cannot understand murder. If you've never believed in much of anything—if you're a dandelion in the gust—you cannot understand. To take poetry seriously is to love one's self. To take poetry seriously is to love one's self loving his brothers and sisters. Predisposed to burn the edifice down. Larry Rios is a murderer. Was a lover. Was loved. Amen.

15. Preach

One fine Sunday afternoon, Larry Rios—no-name poet, lapsed Catholic (though you can't fault him for trying)— leaves church feeling stirred, redeemed, drives downtown, parades to the Alamo where in front of the tourism trap he preaches to passersby words of certifiable boondogglery. Instead of a Bible, he holds loose leaves containing his poems. To his mild astonishment, folks tolerate him. Cowboy hospitality. Only two—a man and woman, homeless—sidle up to our bonehead poet-preacher (Plato's recurrent nightmare) to offer amens. Catholic Revivalism, fancies Larry. Could work. Folks could always use a pick-me-up. (Sweety, Catholic Revivalism *was* the Spanish Inquisition.)

16. Golden Arches

Larry Rios visits McDonald's for French fries. The employee taking his order in the drive-thru asks if he'd like peanut butter to complement them. "Pardon?" says Larry, civilized. "Peanut butter," the kid repeats, affectionate as a sack of throwing stars. Throughout the transaction Larry cracks not one smile. Drives home very sad, actually. Deflated about the state of youth, the country's livelihood. If corporations are people, are they people you'd want in the trenches with you? They're everywhere unflinching far as the eye can see. Fudge, Larry thinks. You know you're getting old when you stop seeing the hilarity in bullshit.

Facebook. Snapchat. Instagram. TikTok around the clock. Big money, big power. Still all alone. Larry Rios' hands unclean, heart searing. News. Shootings. Demented men ripping families apart. The Algorithm sent me. Blood down the school steps. Lamenting in misbegotten prayers—undoing nothing. Ceaseless perversion funneled through smoking barrels. Bedlam. Backpedaling. Repetition. When Larry sinned, it was laser-focused, small-scale. But out there? Worse than nightmares, horrifying fiction. Eyes closed, he wishes now his life were theirs. Our lost tomorrow. Eyes shut, Larry remembers his mother devastated. Why am I an only child? he'd asked. Because one's frightening enough—understand? He'd learn. Amen.

18. Freak-nastiness

Larry Rios spends an afternoon considering myriad variations of human fetishes—time he'll never recover. Eating ravioli off the lower back of a French maid. Making love on horseback (white ponies, of course) off the coast of Costa Rica. Rolling around naked on torn-out pages of the *Twilight* series. Humping upside down shouting "Peter Parker!" at the point of climax. An unspeakable act in front of a Jimi Hendrix poster. Larry says: "Is there no end to our freak-nastiness?" He thinks about Mother Teresa, instantly regrets it. (Aboard every flight, isn't at least one passenger on her way to a funeral?)

19. Comparison

A random guy tells Larry Rios he reminds him of Robert De Niro. Larry resists the urge to say, "You talkin' to me?" Instead, he queries: "From which movie?" The guy raises his hand to his chin, studies Larry a coupla seconds. "All of them, cutie. Somewhere in the middle," he says, making sense only to himself. Larry presses him. "You look like De Niro in a movie he never did," the guy answers, then stumbles off into obscurity, clearly wasted. All Larry thinks is, Cabrón. Then he remembers that wasn't the first time he'd been compared to the illustrious actor.

20. Community

A random guy accosts Larry Rios in the middle of an intense reading session. "Are you a writer or something?" Larry chuckles. "Well," he winds up, "I write, ergo I am." "You published books or something?" Taken aback, Larry reviews his internal Rolodex of sayings, selects: "I'm a work in progress, y'see what I'm saying?" To his relief the guy nods energetically. Larry shows him a poem he'd written titled, "21 tips to better writing." The guy reads aloud but Larry shushes him gentlemanlike. When finished, he whipsers, "Profound." Larry responds: "Merci. Got time for more? Lemme check my back pocket."

21. Surprise

Larry Rios never sees the guy again. Such is often the case in the life and times of our antihero. Connection one day, permanent misdirection the next. This is why—highlight this, dear reader—*the work must always stand for itself.* Always. Amen. An egotistic endeavor, yes, but so is having kids. Larry's a father, by the way. Don't ask him when's the last time he saw his daughter. At this point he's much closer to Yuks the sword-swallowing frog. Though, he does think of her every day. Murderer? Oui. But cold-hearted? Peut-être. All Larry can do is write. Work tirelessly.

22. Sayings

Briefly, an abbreviated list of Larry Rios' sayings: Y'see what I'm saying? Well I'll be tickled. Lord Almighty. You've gotta be fudgin' me. Get outta here. No freakin' way. C'mon, dude. Christ on the cross. There she is. Whoop there it is! Buckets! For reals. No kiddin'. Stop playin'. Yo' mama. You ain't far off. Nitty gritty. Ten-four. Fudgecracker. You know it. It is what it isn't. That's rich. Check's in the mail. Yessir. N'ombre. I gotchu. Oh snap! Come through. Come again? Correctamundo. Then what? You lousy scoundrel. You're the bestest. Peace. Take care. See ya around. Pneumonoultramicroscopicsilicovolcanoconiosis. Yeah. Nope.

23. Traffic

Rush hour has made a richer reader outta Larry Rios. Whereas most folks relegate this dreadful time of day to unleash profanities spoken and inaudible, Larry, prepared, reads. No movement, no problem. Carry on with the story, old sport. Years ago, Larry arrived at the conclusion that life is wasted needlessly on the john, on the road. Always carry a book, Larry'll instruct. You'll find yourself finishing more of them. When it comes to seizing the day, squeezing every last ounce of reading time outta this lime, there's Larry, sweet as lemon. Squeezing, seizing—and about finished with Voltaire. In traffic!

24. Good Literature

Past bedtime, he guesses why French and Argentinian literature tickles his pickle. Because it hardly makes sense. Because straightforward is hemlock to the creative's encephalon. Because on a bad day it smacks the snot outta you and sleeps like a baby. Everyone else lives accordingly, but artists adorn for themselves beautiful deathbeds. Slam bullets down their gullets. Brothers and sisters in pen transmitting to each other a simple memorandum: Live bravely, die stunningly. Larry Rios is transitorily obsessed with Argentine poet Alejandra Pizarnik. Her thousand-yard-stare, suicide eyes, inner death drive. He's convinced he'd been her lacking mentor in another improbable dimension.

25. Buddy

The music of Buddy Holly consistently conjures in Larry Rios' mind the day his father taught him how to play chess. Like this, mijito, his father had instructed. Good, son. Always cherish your queen. Larry would do anything to go back, give him a huge bear hug. He sips black coffee, puts down his pen. Allows Buddy's song to play out. Closes his eyes. Reminisces the night of his wedding, the glowing full moon. "When's the last time you played chess?" Larry asks himself. Suddenly an idea sparks for a poem. Buddy has left the building. Larry's off to the races.

26. Reminder

Let us not forget: Larry Rios is a murderer. Has blood on his hands, under his nails. This is what he learned: life is cheap. Life is cheap. Life's cheap. Larry's heart is an icebox in an incinerator. He's messed up, loco like you. Loses threads like you wouldn't believe. Judges you too. He's got blood on his palms, gum under his desk. Wishes he could go back but has granted himself permission to fail. He'd still choose poetry. Poetry'd still choose him. It's in his genes, less and more than the sum of his blueprint. This: the ecstasy of pathos.

27. Facts

Businessmen bore Larry Rios. Engineers fascinate him. He respects philosophers if they answer "yes" to the question: "Dig poetry?" Larry knew a monsignor who co-wrote a couple of his theology essays in college (who later dropped dead in the middle of a sermon). Larry knew an archbishop who reviled women. Women, naturally, perplex Larry. He's good at making them laugh. Larry's never met a dog that didn't worship him. Dogs're rollovers. Larry names his feisty female betta fish Bruce Lee. Larry undergoes Jeet Kun Do training via YouTube. Knows kung fu. Watch out. Larry watches music videos long into the night.

28. Inspiration

Another somebody asks him, "How do you write so much?" Larry Rios answers: "I write only when inspired, but I'm inspired every day." He steals that line from William Faulkner. But guess what? Faulkner's collecting mold in the cold grave; toasty standing up to gravity is Larry, a pinprick pitched across 46 billion light-years. El Greco continually inspires Larry. His paintings but moreso his biographical particulars. The fish he consumed. His decaying molars. He must've been a pain in the ass, Larry ponders. But he knew the score I'm still searching for. The godawful truth, like his subjects: taffy. Moving on.

29. Memory

A memory replays incessantly—Ma taking him to the grocery store. Holding his hand. Her green dress swaying. Sun shining. Old cars lumbering by. Ice cream sundaes dripping. Happy music filling the air. He's told himself for years it was Etta James. Etta James, the sound of his mother. Swaying green dress. Sweet sugar rush. Bright white teeth. Striking green eyes. He has his mother's eyes. His father's skin. He made a mess of his life. Lost his next of kin. Etta James pummels his heart. Her voice shaped like a hammerfist. He needs what kills him most. Poor Larry Rios.

30. Contradictions

Larry Rios is both a scrupulous man and a wild card. Both a clean freak and a filthy animal. Both a know-it poet and an autodidactic philosopher. A mystery and an open book. A lost lamb and a stubborn mule. Organized and unruly. Black and off-white. Gray and pink. Blue and silly as salamanders. He sucks at soccer but sure can shoot the three-pointer. Gentleman and scholar. Imbecilic and introspective. Diligent, edgy. Ludicrous, practical. Living terror and a marvel. Bibliophile and wannabe detective. A quixotic cannon aimed at your head. A man of many, many contradictions. Larry's none of these things.

31. First Funeral

When Larry Rios was a youngster, he spotted a frog outside his windowsill. Put down his yoyo and approached his parents reluctantly. Keep 'im in your room, they halfheartedly assented. He named him Toad L. Eclipse—best frog this side of the moon! He loved Toad unconditionally. The little amphibian stunk up his room. Upon returning home from school one day, he found Toad unresponsive, paperclip poking out of his lips. Toad: the first pet he buried. The best a boy could do. He delivered a short eulogy. Yuks the sword-swallowing frog isn't an accident. He's the hero Larry never became.

32. Obligation

If you ever run across Larry Rios—he's hard and easy to miss—ask him: "What's the poet's obligation?" Depending on his mood, which side of the bed he rose from, he'll offer you something interesting, guaranteed. "The poet is obligated to no one." Or: "The poet's obligated to obligations." Or: "The poet's obligated to craft." Or: "The poet's obligated to the nitty gritty." Or: "The poet's obligated to disaster." Or: "The poet's obligated to your mother." Then: "Get outta my worldview, interloper." Ol' Larry. Man of copious contradictions. Cold one day, magma the next. One can never be too sure.

33. Conspiracies

Conspiracy theorists were spanked as children, Larry Rios is convinced. He gets a notion to start a blog. (He won't.) One entry about a haunted underground supercomputer called La Llorona. Another: George Washington's hair pressed into one-dollar bills. Another: JFK's incisors turning up in the black market. Another: Dracula roosting in Mexico City. Another: Melville predicting 9/11 in *Moby-Dick*. Another: Tom Hanks subscribing to Satanism. Another: Selena alive cranking out Tejano mixtapes in Liechtenstein. Another: Selena authoring the lyrics to Gnarls Barkley's "Crazy." Another: a sour apple pie bent on agroterrorism. Larry cracks his knuckles. "Cons and piracy," amusedly. "That's rich."

34. Purple Lies

Larry Rios is an expert practitioner of white lies—the lifeblood of the Americas, he believes, for better and for worse. On his way home from work one sunburst evening he ponders what purple lies might look like. Like Prince, he reckons, if Prince had strutted around declaring he was six feet tall. Folks would've eaten that up. Prince was 5'3" and still the High Priest of Pop! Can't nobody handle regal purple lies. Black lights are really purple lights. Purple lies. A novel idea, opines Larry. An idea with nowhere to fly. A pair of wings trapped in the esophagus.

35. Singing

Larry Rios sure can sing—in the shower. Smokey Robinson, Ed Sheeran—move over, there's a new crooner in—the shower. Larry once belted out Ritchie Valens' entire catalog then proceeded to reverse engineer songs in Ritchie's voice that poor Ritchie cannot in this earthly existence enjoy. For example, "Come On, Let's Stay." Larry's water bill rose a horrid seven bucks that month. N'ombre, he'd said, next thing I'm gonna be a wretched starving artist. If Larry should stumble upon a magic genie, one of his three wishes will be to sing like Alicia Keys—in the shower. Audience of one.

36. Collector

Larry Rios is a bibliophile. Collector of dusty narratives. Some of his favorite first editions include: *Intruder in the Dust* by William Faulkner. *Ask the Dust* by John Fante. *V.* by Thomas Pynchon. *The Face of Another* by Kōbō Abe. *Miss Lonelyhearts* by Nathanael West. *Poems from Prison* by Etheridge Knight. *Hopscotch* by Julio Cortázar. *Stoner* by John Williams. A third printing of *The Grapes of Wrath* by John Steinbeck. *Homecoming* by Sonia Sanchez. *White Teeth* by Zadie Smith, signed. *The Orange Eats Creeps* by Grace Krilanovich, signed (despite the novel's steamy incoherence). These are but merely a fraction, dear reader.

37. Resourcefulness

When Larry Rios reads that Kenyan writer Ngugi Wa Thiong'o wrote his first novel, *Devil on the Cross*, on toilet paper whilst imprisoned, one can say that ol' Larry's intrigued. Inspired. The next day, he churns out on eight Post-it notes a manifesto on reverse-reverse assimilation. The day after, another—this one on a fresh banana peel—supporting Catholic Revivalism. Tricky? Indubitably. Sticky? 100%. But probably worth the beating. Larry learns two lessons: manifestos can be written practically on anything—and still, nobody gives a hoot. Who reads? A quarter of the city's illiterate. File 13: wherein the afore-mentioned manifestos lay.

38. Empty

It's a mean world out there when the stars collapse on your head. The city no longer favors your name. The buildings and their boardroom shysters subsume you into their extortion. The trees, leaves—rustling rumors. The land, like hearts of unrequited lovers, a gaping hole filled with time on loan. Walk. Run. Hide in a coffee shop. The roads ahead are warped paths. The grid's anything but copacetic. Cronus wants to chew you alive. Stick you under his worldly gums. Larry Rios takes a final adversarial drag, slings a cigarette into the overgrown night. He's overwhelmed. This too shall pass.

39. Sardines

It occurs to Larry Rios, patting down his cowlick, that the human mind is like a can of jam-packed sardines, but instead of sardines, non sequiturs. Yes, a tin can stuffed with non sequiturs—inane, grotesque, hysterical, often uncooperative thoughts. Meaningless. Or, inexplicably meaningful yet worthless. The human mind, Larry decides, is like a Donald Barthelme short story. The plot: a hundred leagues under the sea, the sea of Jell-O and jet fuel, I too was a fan of Bozo the Clown, I sure do miss those Siamese twins. Lord Almighty, Larry thinks. There goes my tin can being postmodern again.

40. Labyrinth

Bookstore. New Mexico. Sunset. Shelves cast in golden light. *The Labyrinth of Solitude*. Octavio Paz. Prose like a headrush. Kneeling, he drew her in. Kissed her navel. Incredible, he said. See, she whispered. Brushed his hair. Gentle. Broke the news. Eyes glassy. Unblinking. What? he stammered. Kiss it again. Put your ear to it. Suspended. Expanding. Heart hammering. Really? Yes. Yes. Ours. Fingers buried in her waist. Pouring rain. The desert gulped its share. Details we're privy to. The rest his. Some things haunt you a lifetime. Maze of stars. Twinkling light. Somewhere far. Sinking fast. Sweet, sweet dreams, Larry Rios.

41. Modification

Cowlicks emerge on the left side of Larry Rios' head 95% of the time, but this morning, a rare sighting: a right-sided cowlick. As Larry wets his hand and vigorously pats down the anomalous cowlick, he restructures his previous theory. Instead of a can of jam-packed sardines, the human mind is like a skein of yarn—every millimeter of gray matter crammed tightly into a ball. Yanked apart, the dense mass expands into near weightlessness. An illusion. A mere trick. All memories are unreliable, Larry decides. Unstable on their own. We forget the facts; memorize instead *how* we tell the stories.

42. Craving

Larry Rios spots a needle outside his door. The sky's baby blue, clouds like melted marshmallows. "Stop playin'," he says. Looks left, right. No one in sight. Kids chattering in the distance. It's not the needle that scares Larry, what's inside. Every day, the world collapsing, unseaming. Plummeting, shattering. Every day, the story of neglect. Pieces—a puzzle ill-fit for solving. Larry Rios hates popular trends, but it's Tuesday—Taco Tuesday. He can go for bean and cheese with bacon tacos. Dunked in a goblet of salsa verde. He craves them hardcore. His stomach growls animalistically. "Carbohydrates, watch out. I'm coming."

43. Accountability

Because Larry Rios sets atrocious literature aflame, he no longer possesses the first "serious"—air quotes—poems he wrote. After having finished Carlos Fuentes' novella, *Aura,* a voice materialized in Larry's head. Spoke to Johnny-come-lately directly in second person. He couldn't tell if the muse was male, female. (Probably somewhere in between.) It was to you, dear reader, whom Larry addressed his furious batch of debut poetry. He eventually came to acknowledge that second-person poems are cowardly—shirk the poet's accountability, dumps it on your lap. Folks have enough issues of their own to deal with. Larry thinks: I'll lug mine.

44. Beret

The first sign a novelist is taking her novel seriously—she seriously doubts it. Remembers that nobody—hardly anyone—cares. That the giant rock on which we dwell continues its dazzling twirl. That embedded into each of us is deniability—the No. 1 cause for human death. That the fiction writer's burden is heavier than the poet's. That the poet laughs at the novelist and the novelist scoffs at the poet. That the short-story writer isn't even invited to coffee. After Larry Rios stopped writing fiction, he started dreaming of frogs. He gave up his novel and bought a beret. Hooray.

45. Voices

More of Larry Rios' favorite first editions from his library include: *Confessions of a Mask* by Yukio Mishima. A second printing of *The Fountainhead* by Ayn Rand. *With His Pistol in His Hand: A Border Ballad and Its Hero* by Américo Paredes. *Survivors of the Chicano Titanic* by Reyes Cárdenas. *Across the Mutual Landscape* by Christopher Gilbert, signed. *Indian Killer* by Sherman Alexie, signed. *In Watermelon Sugar* by Richard Brautigan (unsigned). *Play It as It Lays* by Joan Didion (unsigned). *Kiss of the Spider Woman* by Manuel Puig (signed and underlined). *Oreo* by Fran Ross. So many voices, so little time.

46. Spitballing

Larry Rios spends a ridiculous evening coming up with names for an imaginary talk show. Needless to say, this is time he'll never recover. *Plain 'n' Stupider with Larry Rios. To The Cheese Moon and Beyond with Larry Rios. Shootin' Straight-ish with Larry Rios. Mosquito Huntin' with Larry Rios. Let It Beyoncé Or Not To Beyoncé with Larry Rios. Tangentially Sexy with Larry Rios. Freddy Krueger Got Fingered with Larry Rios. Zero Yucks Given with Larry Rios. Stanza Split Sunday with Larry Rios. Live From Yo' Mama's House with Larry Rios. Poets 'n' Puppies with Larry Rios.* Puppies. Ah. Que cute.

47. Boxed

With a full stomach and time to kill, Larry Rios strolls downtown by San Fernando Cathedral, notes its Gothic Revival arches, folks exiting the church—a building that'd baffle Christ. He feels the historic landmark's gaze on his back, its ominous watch in broad daylight. His blood goes cold—this unfathomable metropolis. An hour later he writes a poem on a Starbucks napkin under the shade of an oak tree. By Larry's standards it's abysmal. He crumples the napkin. He's hungry again. Parched. The show goes on in this small-town big city where death by flying suicides remains a bloodcurdling possibility.

48. Anonymous

On a dozen or so scraps of legal pad paper he handwrites this sentiment: *Maybe you need to hear this, but today wouldn't have been the same without you.* No initials. He folds each anonymous note twice and waits for a windy day. It's Saturday morning when he goes to a park and launches his notes in the air, one by one. One by one, the refreshing spring breeze sweeps them up and away. Littering, incontestably, but Larry Rios likes to think this a small act of kindness in a shipwrecked subsistence. Tonight, he falls asleep a little bit faster. Drools.

49. Competitiveness

During his lunchbreak Larry Rios drives to a gas station and while filling up his car notices on the asphalt a crushed cigarette, a flattened June bug and three heart-shaped Valentine's candies. "Christ on the cross," he blurts out. Back at work his mind goes haywire generating titles to theoretical poetry collections he'll never write: *Vanity Unleaded*, *Bug Guts & Sweethearts*. Art everywhere. Art are the tangents we care for. Tangents and distractions. Poets the Great Distractors; painters and photographers: the Great Detractors. Larry's salty. His competitive streak's showing. Chill, Larry. Chill. Take it down a skosh. Signe de la croix.

50. Clarity

To be clear, Larry Rios doesn't really hate folks; he just gets super frustrated with them, is sometimes part of the problem though he's loath to admit it. Larry's no Daniel Plainview (of the superb *There Will Be Blood*); he's an eccentric centrist Marxist with a thumping core. He's deeply sensitive to electric impulses, mercurial mammal—hot one day, iceberg the next. He isn't cold-hearted. He's irascible, rational. Repeatedly revolted by mass hysteria. He's 10% sheep, 90% wolf. He occasionally loses it. He's capable of murder. He's Mr. Fix It. He's none of these things. He's made his bed for today.

51. Assistance

Leaving Jim's Restaurant after editing poems while indulging in coffee and pie, Larry Rios encounters outside the entrance an obese wheelchaired woman. Cigarette dangling from her lips, she asks Larry for a light. "Allow me," he says. Suave. The woman can't decide if the gentleman reminds her of her ex-husband or estranged son. For minutes she explains to Larry her bodily dysfunctions, her life's chief regrets. Larry listens, nods accordingly. He gifts her his lighter clinging to the last of its butane. "Have a blessed night, ma'am." Driving home, her green dress and immeasurable misery are broken records in his mind.

52. Wakes

Monday afternoon. Clear blue skies. Birds warbling. Folks congregated in the streets. A woman's trill enchanting the crowd. Gospel number. Suffering into sweet wine. Hot food lines. The starving nourished. Old men busting jokes. Blooming women dancing with dates. A fiddler tapping his foot. A saxophonist fingering his brass to tears. Larry Rios wakes slowly. Head pounding. Room shrouded in deep black. He swallows an aspirin. Sips water from his hand. Shuts his eyes under the covers. Forgets the other world. Song and dance. Tomorrow will be a struggle. Another bout. For now, he must wait. Wait. Wait to fade out.

53. Sweats

Barbara Jane Reyes' *For the City That Nearly Broke Me* proves overstimulating for Larry Rios. Upon closing the chapbook, he speaks in tongues to the sun. Tongue out, sunlight-dilated pupils. Muddy green eyes, his mother's. Snapping out of it: "Nice to see ya today, Mr. Sol. Gets lonely up high I bet." With Yuks the sword-swallowing frog off his conscience, he remembers bills are due. After submitting payments online, Larry—having not lifted nor run in weeks—hits the gym. Stretches his arms, hamstrings. Holds a plank for a shaky minute. Breaks himself to rebuild, visualizing attainable abs he'll never obtain.

54. Geometry

He gulps down the last of his juice, reluctantly relinquishes forcing out more poems; his mind isn't in it today. Half a beat slow. Then a miniscule miracle—it strikes Larry Rios promptly clear as mud that triangles taste—yes, taste— like the color orange, shrewd and citric. A trio of triplets ooze from his pen. He imagines the great poet Lorca contemplating the swelling Spanish countryside, his leftist politics marshalling him to inevitable destruction. "Now there's a real firecracker!" Larry exclaims. He concludes that ovals taste purple—lackadaisical and bittersweet— lazy and pleased. This is how poetry incubates. Mystery solved.

55. A for Effort

Let it be known by all who grace this green, blue, blood-soaked earth that Larry Rios can't dance. He can sing, belt out smooth tunes, croon, but the gift of groove didn't transfer to his hips, his inner weather balloon. That ever stop him from trying? You can catch Larry on select Saturday mornings swinging stiffly to "Be My Baby" by The Ronettes. Soundtrack of his life—cradle to grave—rolling out on grainy film like the opening to Scorsese's *Mean Streets*. Scarcely do melodies contain mortality's vastness. If you can't sing, dance. If you can't dance, you must be dead.

56. Fishbowl

Years ago, during a warm breezeless starlit night, insects buzzing, Lucia led their ascent to the rooftop where they laid on their backs, gazed into the neverending universe. Feeling disjointed, he initiated conversation, and was soon spellbound by the sound of her voice, the cosmos sharing deep dark secrets, the sensation of being blindfolded in an orchestral echo chamber. No sooner did he slip into dream than he awoke with his head on her chest, shirt damp with sweat, the sky a humongous fishbowl. You snore beautifully, she said. Then he kissed her with the word *liar* dissolving under his tongue.

57. Grit

Another rough night for Larry Rios. Not nearly as stormy as for the sick, the dying. Still, when heavy, swollen to near bursting, Larry voyages inward—another chat with James Baldwin. "Jimmy, I donno know why I'm coming to you again—you know nothing about post-1987—but I need somebody to talk to (the mirror and wall notwithstanding)." Baldwin rubs his temple folds, says fiercely, "My biggest regret, baby, is I did plenty of writing, lotsa arguing—but damned if I couldn't've slammed more grit into it!" Hard times call for steel sledgehammers—"with rubber grips," blurts a voice just outta focus.

58. Swimming

So what does our guy do? He hunkers down. Gets busy. Creates from scratch some of the worst verse imaginable—onward. Who gives a crap? Nobody reads anyway. A poet's work is never done. He can hardly be content, cannot fall outta love with disillusionment. He must swim in obscure lakes until his arms and lungs clock out. Until he slams into a branch. The tree of life. Larry Rios pictures his work on a dusty bookshelf. A neglected library. Dead names. Disembodied voices. Delusions of grandeur—the poets' lifeblood. Drink up. Swallow. How easily everything can burn down, Larry knows.

59. Binding

Larry Rios' definitions of poetry: 1) Subterranean lyrical odyssey. 2) Extraterrestrial solitary exigency. 3) Lonesome delivery of vital dispatch. 4) Firepool of serpent-honey word whippings. Ol' Larry, artsy fartsy flexing perplexing. Why basic when you can extra? He'd texted his buddy Nelson to see how he was holding up. Nelson was a police officer. Coupla years in the department. Idealistic. Young-ish enough to still trust folks. He'd enjoyed occasional coffee chats with Nelson. Picked his brain on the latest he'd read. Literature—sometimes a binding force. Keep your enemies close, your cop friends closer. Community. Build bridges in case of fire.

60. Poetry Voice

Much irks Larry Rios but little quite like "poetry voice," that diaphragmatically challenged cadence that stretches five minutes into fifteen. Larry once heard a celebrated local poet read his critically acclaimed work in poetry voice. Five minutes in, Larry peaces out. An audience member gasps. He's booed, the hooligans, which justifies an unburdened night's sleep. He wishes sleep was as restful as poetry voice was drawn out. This isn't to say that Larry didn't struggle shedding poetry voice from his practice. Bad habits're goblins in your hemoglobin. He's got his share of problems, alright. Ninety-nine problems. But poetry voice ain't one.

61. Eye

Fires from Hell raze, the wind sweeping across the land mercilessly. No freedom in sight. The earth craves rebirth again. The rug yanks. Fulfill your duty into the cracks. You're mostly water. Sometimes you don't want to get up. Can't. Everywhere scorch and dripping gore. Poison. Flood. Guttural shouts. Ravaged vocal cords. The prophets cry for their messiahs. Saviors—heroes. Tunnels of light. Suffering must be worth the glory. Behold—the poet's work is never done. He's shattered—tattered, battered, gravity roosting on his nerve endings. He forces movement. Up. Atlas' bastard. Bloodshot gaze fixed on the cyclone's eye. Staring contest.

62. Fading

Ribbit ribbit goes the frog ribbit ribbit croak of God ribbit ribbit foggy smog ribbit ribbit dookie dog ribbit ribbit poke a log ribbit ribbit sings Yuks the sword-swallowing … wakes. Soaked sheets. "Dang," he mumbles. Stumbles out of bed. Splashes cold water on his puffy face. You're whacked out, daddio, he thinks. Simmer down. Easy, now. Easy, boy. Easy Larry. You got work in a few. Unanswered emails, voicemails. Did I check the mail? Bills, bills, bills. Everybody begging for something. Highway bums. Got change to spare? Who won the game last night? Nobody played last night. Everybody's somewhere fading.

63. Torrent

Rain hammers against his windows. Thunder renders him restless. He flicks on his nightlamp and for eons shy of eternity pens a poem. For reasons undefined—poetry's nature—it's about his long-dead uncle. It's the age of airborne toxins and Larry Rios is locked down—locked up and working agitatedly. Unblinking. Transcribes his poem onto a Word document then from his phone reads it aloud in his bathroom. Episodically he glances skyward. To whom is my poem addressed? he wonders. Myself? My uncle? The living? The murdered? The silenced? Silence. The storm's passed. Outside, salientian cries of guardians. The postpluvial splendor.

64. Cardio

Larry Rios runs. Larry Rios runs fast. Larry Rios runs away fast. Larry Rios runs away fast listening to "Runnin'" by The Pharcyde. It's the age of persecution complex and Larry huffs and puffs, runs away fast from the still-fresh visage of last night's visit. The Snake-Haired Lady, after all these years, hasn't tired of checking in on him. Her two, three questions he leaves unanswered. He can't tell if his eyes are open when she emerges. Her black sockets, black teeth, stench puncturing like needles. Best to run away for now, Larry Rios. Run away fast. Call it cardio. Routine.

65. Bubbly

"Poetry's the ooold-time religion, it's the oooold-time religion, it's the ooooold-time religion and it's good en-ough for meee!" Larry Rios belts from his comfy couch, an Appalachian music deity having blessed him temporarily with simple clean lyricism, woodsy whimsy from a bygone era—an enchantingly bubbly mood to generate the purest Yuks the sword-swallowing frog poems—fitting given that Yuks is blissfully depressed, affable as any tormented Parisian mime. Speaking of—Larry dated a former mime once. Tina Sandiego—blithely opinionated, lithe, motor-mouthed extrovert. Deaf in one ear. Her first questions to him: Dig poetry? Croissants? Can you speak louder, please?

66. Obsession

Larry Rios hasn't forgiven Carl Bruner from *Ghost*. Y'know, the evildoer portrayed by Tony Goldwyn who gets dragged unceremoniously to Hell. Whenever Larry sees Tony Goldwyn screenwise, he's seeing backstabbing Carl— doomed shoes propelling him astray. Larry's obsessed with pain evermore; obsessed with obsessive authors whose literature features obsessive characters. Bolaño's *2666*, Sabato's *The Tunnel*, Bioy Casares' *The Invention of Morel*, Lispector's *The Hour of the Star*, even Hornby's *Juliet, Naked*. As our lens narrows in on Latin American writers, what in their water induced such scorched-earth fanaticism? Zooming out: What's more American than obsession? Frank Lloyd Wright designs? Apple pie?

67. Scream

A quick temperature check on social media informs Larry
Rios that the state of things is like Edvard Munch's *The
Scream*. Uneasy and wobbly, murky and despairing; lots
of loud noise, extremely piercing. Larry considers the little
he's read about the Norwegian Modernist painter—an
insecure wreck who'd nearly drunk himself to death before
a late-career spiritual turnaround. If that rascal could do
it, anyone can, Larry thinks. Although, and he's loath to
admit this, screaming into one's pillow is pretty freakin'
purifying. If you're ever feeling hideous or lethargic—
especially lethargic—grab a pillow and emancipate your
throat into it.

68. Whirlpool

Larry Rios, lying supine on his couch, enters a psychological loophole. Or rather, a mental spiral. He spirals: If I consider running—and Lord knows I ought to after that last Butterfinger bar—then I must, eventually, envision myself walking. Or worse, sleeping. And if I consider sleeping, then I must envision myself waking. Or worse, breathing. And if I consider breathing, then I must envision myself choking. Or worse, suffocating. And if I consider dying … and so forth. It takes Larry going on a run, ironically, for him to snap this vicious impervious whirlpoolish cycle. Good golly, Miss Molly.

69. Dangling Participles

Larry Rios decides that dangling participles make poetry more sufferable. *Trudging through the fires of Mordor / the smoke alarm was going crazy.* "Aha, the power of stanza," Larry declares, replacing the battery on his smoke alarm. "To subvert the action of stone clauses: stanza. To loophole the Tungsten grammarians: stanza. To believe the smoke alarm trudges through Mordor's fires, not the speaker: stanza!" Poetry attracts only the troublemakers—punks, Larry concludes. *One evening I shot a platypus / in my undies.* What more need be writ? *Reading the beginning / I ride the end.* Sound the alarm. Now we're cooking.

70. Ouroboros

Pardon Larry Rios' French, but: "The city's covered in [expletive]!" Proximally—odor, fungus, must, dust, dander, doo, effluvium, soot, exhaust, grime, sludge, crud, muck, goo, ooze, funk, gunk, scum ad nauseum. Nausea. Forget the sights; it's the stink that sinks your brain folds. Wakey-wakey, smell the egg-rot and bakey. The Dark Ages never ended, just got steamier—global roasting. We're the ouroboros unfinished with itself; we're not hungry, we're saving room for cupcakes. These platitudes belong solely to Larry Rios. He sees somebody toss a plastic bottle outta their car, their bumper sticker an ichthys encircling the phrase: *Pray in Everything*.

71. RHCP

Larry Rios is on his merry way to buy milk, instant coffee, sparse sundries, when "I Could Die for You" by the Red Hot Chili Peppers plays. Thirty seconds later its opening lyrics are all it takes for him to know its the tenderest song he's heard. *Something inside the cards / I know is right / Don't want to live / somebody else's life.* Somewhere in the horizon, Anthony Kiedis is hurting badly, eternally. The pain of longing never fully fades. About Kierkegaardian anguish: It's only meant to happen to you. Live inside you wordless forever and a day. Amen.

72. Schrödinger's Mirror

He can't recall where he'd read the phrase *wilderness of mirrors* to describe North America's psyche, so experiment- and antic-primed Larry Rios opens his medicine cabinet, angles its smaller mirror to face the larger one, resulting in seemingly infinite shrinking mugshots of Larry Rios. A relentless hall of Larry Rioses. Only someone in dire straits—a prostrate state—would attempt to try to better understand North America's overextended essence. Only someone who's a masochist, whose identity's desperately compromised. Creative Writing Rule Numero Uno: Mirrors are stand-ins for skeletons in the closet. If he kills the bathroom light, is Larry simultaneously dead-and-alive?

73. Suspicious Sunday

Bruce Lee, Larry Rios' betta, nibbles her flakes as Larry contemplates becoming another man. He was another man before the man he is today; when has transformation ever arrested the act of metamorphosis? Metamorphosis: the original gateway drug. Chances are, if you pass through one gate, you've passed through 'em all. Prices went up on fish food. Larry's dismayed. "It's expensive to be captive," he says, "a metaphor for everything." Bruce Lee appears unfazed by Larry's insight—keyword: *appears*. The whine of distant buzzsaws. Disruptive construction, uninterrupted. You never know who's tuning in, soaking it all up on a suspicious Sunday.

74. Pyro

Poetry died this morning, and she's dead. Throw on your beret, Larry Rios. Let dangle your cigarette. You've resuscitatin' to do in that nasty jumble out yonder once pointed to by mass murderers turned to statues. Fudge the police, stimulus checks—you're a madhatter surgeon. Revive the departed with your sharpened quill—giant cleaver—clippers—your godforsaken Toledo saber. Charlemagne's Joyeuse, Arthur's Excalibur. You hail from a fiery line of conquerors; most of us do at this point, choosing to forget; meanwhile, you secure your name on rock, paper, collective memory. Murderer, yes, but also firestarter. Where there's smoke, there's hope.

75. Paranoid Sunday

It's a paranoid Sunday and he writes and writes and writes and writes. Writes, sips coffee, pees, deletes, writes, removes volumes from his bookshelf. Julia de Burgos. José Martí. Sandra Cisneros. Walt Whitman. Lorca. Paz. Langston. Rupi Kaur! "Speak," Larry Rios summons them, the storm of translations, near-exact significations, implications, vortex of the living dead, the dead-alive— surges of voice smashed against the barges. This is how one ignites himself. Marks himself a worthy target. Lone intended audience. Poetry—solitudinous but may trigger earthquakes. Beware. He sits on his floor and writes and writes and writes and deletes. Deletes some more.

76. Indecipherable

Anytime he stops by the McNay, Larry Rios gets as close up as possible to El Greco's *Head of Christ*. The painting's dimensions, height and width both barely longer than a foot, somehow, to Larry, make it appear larger than life. Larry wrote three poems inspired by the painting, the best of which to him, titled, "Slanted eyes in prayer," is a love poem to his ex, but with his estranged daughter in mind. After critiquing the painting numerously, Larry concludes three things: Christ's watery eyes are indecipherable, the messiah's agony is palpable, and El Greco is a trickster—a cobra.

77. Game

Part of Larry Rios' practical (albeit unsettling) charm is his partiality for thinking like a Frenchman. Or rather, an existentialist. "Suppose without God tickling himself in the clouds, the universe is the result of an enigmatic—yet meaningless—eruption in panoramic directions, ultimately explained—nay, codified—by arithmetic. Ergo, sin is mythical—i.e., manmade—and murder's reality is a pinhole on the ol' celestial belt." Larry can't shake the perception that the examined life is a game revered by critics but played by few. "The ratings blow," he adds, "and there's no uncrueling this cruel program." Bruce Lee swims in circles.

78. Neologism

Tonight, telescopes spy the shy stars; meanwhile, Larry Rios invents a verb. Pangs of nostalgia make another guest appearance, activating in him the notion to cook: Hamburger Helper Stroganoff it is. Side Caesar salad. After two stroganoffalicious servings, Larry scoops leftovers into a Tupperware container, plays from his phone "The Whole World" by OutKast, volume cranked up, Crip Walks toward his fridge, Tupperware in hand. His left knee momentarily gives out, Larry pratfalling, Tupperware flying slow motion—Zeno's rocket—before exploding across his living room carpet. "Fudgecracker," he says. "I *stroganoffed* my fudgin' mancave." The newfangled verb leaves an oleaginous voicestain.

79. Smooth Criminal

You're probably wondering how Larry Rios knows how to Crip Walk. Get this: unpaid red-light camera ticket. Just kidding. Cop stops him one evening for going nine miles over the speed limit. It was his last disgruntled day on duty and he was in a lawless mood to cite Larry (expired license and all) for reckless driving. "You're fudgin' me." "I fudge you not." A night in the slammer. Larry's stint: kicking it for nine hours with a dealer named Jay—"Homies call me Great Gatsby." Gatsby takes Larry for a closeted pimp. Gatsby C-Walks: a truth, dare. Larry learning quick.

80. Probability

Sipping piping hot caffeine this brightening morning, squinting Larry Rios—mind Rubik's Cubing with no resolution in mind—opens his laptop, flings thoughts onto a villainously blank page. Wonders, How many sword-swallowing frogs would it take for one to produce a poem about an ignoramus dubbed Larry Rios writing poems about a sword-swallowing frog called Yuks? The first paragraph of Genesis from the Catholic Bible? Lyrics to any Bob Dylan song? God knows (Pascal's Gambit dictating that it's safer, simply, to believe). The list goes on. Earth's shaped like a globe—most of us knowing supplied only by faith. Dig? Preach.

81. Southerner

The sun disappearing behind a bank of mountainous clouds. Larry Rios thinks of the Greek poet Sappho, how the same sunsets for her had once inspired visions of golden chariots. He thinks about his grandfather on horseback, dust swirling across the old Mexican village. Larry's hit with outlandish inescapability that he's a Southern writer—a Chicano poet, have mercy. He once debated a buddy who'd believed there was a difference between Southern and Texas writers; to Larry, it mattered not one iota on this toyish sphere. Mere semantics. Homer, Larry McMurtry, Flannery O'Connor—don't matter. Sunshine toasts us all the same.

82. Callback

Unbeknownst to him, he'd texted his cop buddy Nelson at the worst time. Days later, he heard back. (If a text message falls in the woods—) Nelson, over the phone: Sorry, brother, something came up. Yeah? Anything juicy? Can't really get into it, Nelson said, y'know how that goes. Say less, fam. Coffee, though? Only if it's my treat, he replied. Before they hung up, he asked Nelson abruptly: It's nothing about a murder or any unusual disappearances, right? A brief pause stretching spacetime; then, No. And would that pass polygraph inspection? A Nelson-sized chortle. Cop humor—gets 'em everytime.

83. Symphony

Seventy degrees. Cool crisp breeze. The mockingbirds mock, crows crow. Larry Rios hikes slow, watches oak trees and mountain cedar sway leisurely to nature's will. He lifts his strong arm, extends it toward the trees, waves it left, right, west and east, over and over as though conducting the pulse of the green synchronous motion. He's unaware, uncaring of what passersby may think. His caring has jack squat to do with thinking. He's in his world. Of the world, yet rejecting its arbitrary expectations. He recognizes the hardship in making memories alone. Hence his spontaneous symphony, crickets hardly silencing their phones.

84. Arrival

The first time The Snake-Haired Lady appeared was in the village in Mexico. His grandfather shut the door, the walls and floorboards tinting themselves in the moon's bluish albedo. From the corner of the room, she approached the foot of his bed. He thought maybe she was his grandfather's comadre, the sweet woman who made rosaries and bread. Her mouth opened; his body froze, burned. Her hair floated, hissed; his ear scavenged by her tongue. (What did she hear inside?) He awoke naked. Panicked. The licking language of pain. Prayed never to see her again. To never return to old Mexico.

85. Motown

Maybe he's loco, but Larry Rios is convinced that "I Can't Help Myself (Sugar Pie Honey Bunch)" by The Four Tops is the saddest song ever. Motown Records sure knew how to scramble folks' emotions. The formula: messy hearts make messy ears. The song resonates joyousness but belies the throbbing loss of perpetual alteration. Every second—another vanished. Try stopping it. Shoot, Larry muses, all music is soul music. It's what I die and relive for. Dear reader, from this angle, Larry's heaving. Laughing or weeping. He's going at it. It's going at him full speed. "We're a mess!" he screams.

86. Safe

Here's a weird one, eldritch reader. After a conference in Houston, Larry Rios drops by a Half Price Books to let rush-hour traffic die down. He'll get home when he gets home. He purchases works he'd already read, he loves 'em so much. Soon, he discovers a cursive inscription in the middle of the old mass-market paperback copy of *Giovanni's Room* he'd copped cheap. *For Bill(y) Styron—Yours till the gritty lady sings. James Baldwin. P.S. Don't sell this book.* "Lord Fudgecracker Almighty!" the definition of a holler. The book rests—among other documents—safely in a safe under his bed.

87. Clarity Revisited

Larry Rios would categorize his relationship with living poets as an experiment without a hypothesis. At several open mics he was received benignly, seemingly. But up on that bright hot stage he could feel their cold glares undressing him: a slimy, avaricious bipedal inside a terrarium. Afterwards: sympathy applause. He once made the error of setting up a poem longer than it took him to read it. It was like explaining a joke, which was like dissecting a frog: better understood but superdead at the end. These days, Larry doesn't want his poetry understood. He's improving at becoming clear as mud.

88. Preview

Larry Rios isn't agreeable, disagreeable. He'd disagree. He fancies himself a fellow of hard science, a free-associating dissolvent, a unit of bitter pleasure. (He's still hashing this out). Show him your hand. He'll show you his mean streak. He isn't a dog named Buddy, nor Yuks the sword-swallowing frog. He likes magic cards. Loathes Magic: The Gathering™. He's seasick from content. Signs. Shifting blots. The youth can't resist handstands. Animal masks. Present-tense captions. Hashtags. *#althuman*. All that prancing. *All that murdering and fucking, and no sons?* Matt Damon to Jack Nicholson, *The Departed*. We'll come back later (Chapter 116) to Jack.

89. Mask

A mask embodies deception on two layers—outside and underneath. The face is a mask we decorate with fuzz and paint. Every other day, Larry Rios shaves. Every few months, permits his dark beard to blossom. Aesthetics personify duplicity on three layers—outside, underneath and within. Poems are the lies the inconstant heart sings to the gullible eyes. A journey. Sprinkles them with seeds of delight and decay. Weeds burst through the dermis. Pesky blackheads on red-brown skin. Sheath in parts cratered, partly smooth as ivory—deceptive circumference. Scrubbed regularly, troubled subcutaneously. Powered by what prevails as mystery. Wince and abide.

90. Confidence

One's willingness to take on—to face, brawl with, stand against—his fragility relies upon his ability to stand up straight. In clinical psychology the literature shows that straightness—posture, not sexual orientation, rigorous reader—is a confidence-exuding stance. Confidence: a characteristic of vulnerability. In feministic parlance, to be vulnerable is to be confident is to be—in waves—like a woman. Confidence: baring one's chest proudly to the proliferating haters. Larry Rios loved his lovely mother. Standing straight, our undesirable father wonders about his daughter night and day. All the confident mortals sashaying, bypassing resevoirs of knowledge under their noses.

91. Binary

Larry Rios wakes up on the wrong side of bed today. Therefore, his mind is limited to binary rationale. He reasons: You're either one of two kinds of folks—you speak with commas, or you don't. You speak in proper sentences or you don't. He reconsiders: Unless you're mute. In which case you either think with commas, or you don't. Or it could be, he reassesses, that all consciousness is frantic and offensive and incessant like a stomped-on anthill. "Hmm," Larry hmms. He can't say anything with 100% certainty. He certainly can say 100% anything. He's determined to be himself fractionally.

92. Unsafe

Somewhere along the way, the noun *safe space* infiltrated its way into the dictionary, as words must. Hear that? Intestinal rumblings. The spacious world, mankind's saga—100% of it—finger-painted in sapiens' blood. Which spaces aren't unsafe? Universities? Health centers? Chapels? Bedrooms? Graveyards? Bomb shelters? Wombs? Of any ostensible refuge, universities, especially, ought to be populated with folks equipped to weaponize budding heads against interminable horrors of human ritual. Uncategorizable marginalia. Nonbinary histories. Yet the mission's failed pre-takeoff. Misleading statements leading well-intentioned kids to preventable slaughter. Charging 'em tuition. Sayonara. Thoughts and prayers. The problem? Inexhaustible subproblems. Someone needs a nap.

93. Hypotheticals

Larry Rios can rewrite the history of the world. Can stay in bed all day long. Can forge poems about Wittgenstein through Yuks the sword-swallowing frog's spyglass. Can fancy joining the circus, visualize his last breath from Proxima Centauri b's viewpoint. Can starve his betta, scratch *double-murderer* off his bucket list (though anyone over the age of five years old is a double-murderer at minimum). Can walk twenty thousand steps a day and arrive no closer to becoming a better father. He can run, he can hide. Try to cover his hide. He's guilty on all counts of living. Court's adjourned.

94. Beget

This is an almost true story. An almost untrue story. Money makes miracles. Miracles make money, seawater, ticking stars. Larvae, straight white teeth. Larry Rios takes off work, works from home. One foot in front of the other. One word following another—description of a face—The Snake-Haired Lady's: forehead long as desert. Skin like wolf-trodden snow. Tongue black as forest rot. Sometimes he thinks he'll escape. Avoid Hell's lash. His novel life reduced to a monostich in her dangerous gaping mouth. I forgot to mention something earlier, prevailing reader: miracles beget miracles, but they don't resolve the consequence of time.

95. Tango

Larry Rios once tangoed with Fate and Fortune, stunning creatures from opposite ends of the ether. But since tango's designed for two passionates—it takes two to tango—the logic of Larry's quasi-mythical poem was busted. However, Larry, a poet of quick solutions, titled his poem, "Tango for three." Boom. Conundrum solved. The thing about Chicano poetry is it giggles in the face of guidelines. Mocks the house of order and euphony. Chicano poetry's queendom: acknowledgement then disregard; straight lines then buried stanzas; catacombs and sword-swallowing frogs. Larry considers getting a replacement pet toad. Decides his betta fish is plenty sufficient.

96. Autodidacticism

Question: How does one possibly become an autodidactic philosopher? Answer: Study under a didactic philosopher, possibly. In university daze Larry Rios took several western philosophy courses taught by curly-headed professor Maximillian Masterson who, throughout lectures, weaved the tale—cliffhangers intentional—of his scholarship in Jerusalem. A listless then-Baptist Oklahoman craving meaningful congregation, kinship, trysts, betrayals. Wandering the Temple Mount befriending runaway wives of imams. Playing Texas hold 'em with vulgar Hasidic Jews. Wagering his pitiable soul equally with peasants. Said the agnostic academic: I learned we're exactly right-sized—now who's ready for some Übermensch? Turn to page thirteen, you unseasoned pipsqueaks.

97. Half-Poems

Attending a Billy Collins reading—or someone else's, whose? the details don't matter—Larry Rios decides the key—no, the recipe, the formula—to writing excellent poems is to write half-poems. Half-true poems, in other words, akin to half-furnished rooms allowing readers a cozy move-in, room to spread, lounge. Poor or decorous poems are museums—pretty artifacts abound, but move along, and don't touch anything. You break it you buy. Fantastic poems are dorm rooms—so many knickknacks to tack up, so little real estate, each item carrying tremendous weight. A torpedo hits Larry: exotic poems are the ones left unwritten.

98. Blasphemy

"Sip. Sip. Sip. Sip. Sipsipsip." Repetition of the slender verb. Soft reverberations on breastbone melding into heartbeats. Words giving up their husks, converting, eventually, to fickle air's caprice. Larry Rios chants for one minute—a minute that seems to burst the boundaries of spatiotemporal jurisdiction any way sliced. A breach, a leak. He prays, "Blessed is he who's thirsty and bends his breath in the name of the Lord. You out there, Ma, listening? Sip. Sip. Sip. Sip. Sipsipsip. Amen." Larry isn't a regular practitioner of prayer or Zen Buddhism. He spills coffee on his Bible and expects no one's lenience.

99. Spaceman

Larry Rios, extraordinarily unextraordinary poet. A man at war with himself. A man-o-war poet. Which came first: Archaeopteryx or the egg? Cats or dogs? Spanish or Portuguese? Two of these brainteasers can be cracked with history. What's your story? Her story? His story? Me, I don't make the rules; I just write rubbish down. Right or wrong. Black or white. Innocent and criminal. Stars are the universe's pockmarks. No, pearls. Orion's Belt is God's pearl necklace. No, choker. Because God is emo and gushes warm monsoon tears. The moon's a satellite. Larry's a spaceman. A tortured astronaut of verse and murder.

100. Other Larry

Larry Rivers, American painter. Born Yitzroch Loiza Grossberg, Aug. 17, 1923, the Bronx. Parents: Jewish immigrants from Ukraine. Died Aug. 14, 2002, New York City. Liver cancer. Changed name to Larry Rivers in 1940 working as jazz saxophonist. Larry Rivers and the Mudcats. Studied at Juilliard School of Music with Miles Davis. Started painting in 1945. Merged non-objective, non-narrative art with narrative and objective abstraction. Considered Godfather of Pop art. Married in 1945. One son. Remarried in 1961. Two daughters. Romantically linked to poet Frank O'Hara in late 1950s. Relation to Larry Rios: none, albeit a few particulars—chiefly, certain death.

101. First Punks

Allen Ginsberg once called Arthur Rimbaud "the first punk" of poetry. Not just of poetry but the whole world. If you ask me, I politely disagree. Here're some premier punk alternatives: Socrates. Alexander the Great. Joan of Arc. Napoleon. Genghis Khan. Christopher Columbus. Ivan the Terrible. La Malinche. Mary Antoinette. Mary Shelley (heartwarmingly so). Rasputin. Wu Zetian, the only empress to sit on China's throne, who, legend has it, left behind so many bodies they clogged up the mighty Yellow River. Whoa. That's beyond punk. But what isn't these days? These splendid elegiac days drowned in the bottomless black of night.

When exactly did Larry Rios become master of language? No longer enslaved to the word? No longer constrained by spent breath and printed ink? Definitely after the fall of the Third Reich. And definitely after the Spanish conquest of the Aztecs. But definitely before the second coming of Christ. And definitely before the first shot that would ring in World War [redacted]. Close reader, if it's accuracy you seek—irrefutable laser precision—this account thrives somewhere between heaven and Atlantis. Hades and El Dorado. Everywhere and nowhere. Multiple planets. On the moon of our moon in the penumbra of this species.

103. Another Chat

Another chat with James Baldwin, whose spirit likely emanates from the signed paperback Larry Rios keeps locked away under his bed. Because literature—mouthpiece of the deceased—speaks to us always, always. "Long time no see, pretty baby. How's it swingin'?" "Gee whiz, Jimmy, I'm feeling something awful lately." "I know exactly of what you speak. But do spill." "My life force … it's slipping. Sliding through my fingers. All the secrets mounting … crushing my mind palace." "White man gettin' ya?" "N'ombre, Jimmy. C'mon, dude, be for reals." "Apologies. What I meant to say was: honesty shall set you back."

104. Uncomfortable

He'd written a godawful story about the most terrifying place on earth—the world's center—when his phone finally buzzed. Yo! Sorry for calling late. Saw your text earlier but got sucker-punched by work. What's proper, brother? Everything gravy? Doing alright, just here polishing a turd of a piece. How's my favorite pig doing? Been bananas, dude. No rest for the wicked protecting and serving the beautiful, treacherous people. My man, his commendation, before adding: Remember that lil' convo we had the other day? Awkward silence. About looking up your ex-wife? Correctamundo. Brother, seriously? Course not. Would that pass polygraph analysis?

105. Twos

Briefly, the premise of Nathanael West's 1931 debut novel, *The Dream Life of Balso Snell*: Immature Greek poet stumbles upon the Trojan Horse, infiltrates via *rear* exit, encounters biographer's biographer's biographer and a flea-saint who'd snacked on the flesh of Christ. On Dec. 22, 1940, West, an awful driver, ran a stop sign in California, killing him and his wife. The previous day, in Hollywood, F. Scott Fitzgerald drank himself to death. That's how they flicker out sometimes: in twos. After his uncomfortable call with Nelson, he wondered, Who will succeed my demise? Also: Will anyone dare to jot it down?

106. The Score

Whenever Larry Rios marvels at someone's library, especially his own, he's not marveling at the books that're there, but rather the books that could be there. "Dang," he says aloud while shaving, "what a sad-sap way to occupy space in this hamster wheel." To Larry, the unremitting heartache of existence is like a Charles Bradley song. No, too melodic—more like Christopher Nolan's *Memento*—intense, dissonant. Intensely dissonant. Dissonantly intense. "N'ombre," Larry says, wiping foam off his chin, "quit screwin' around with words like you know the score." Now El Greco, that dude knew the score. But also, motherfudging Christopher Nolan.

Wednesday evening. Seconds after penning the line, *I am the daughter of Lorca*, he hears the familiar pounding upstairs: basketball dribbles. A disturbance, but all's well. "Attagirl," Larry Rios whispers. Last winter, retrieving mail, he'd spotted her outside performing crossover drills between cones. Nice handles, he'd said. But what about your jay? You'll lose your quickness someday, your hops, but never your jumper. Buckets! You can't win alone. Oh, and limit your screen time. Phones steal souls. Peace. Unbeknownst to Larry, the youngin had won a three-point contest at her school. By day, she was straight-A prodigy in an e-girl outfit.

108. Simple Question

Sooner or later, every soldier and writer must ask themselves the simple question: What do you sincerely hope to accomplish by spilling blood and words? (One in the same.) One can say Larry Rios is expert at no crafts. One can say Larry Rios dons bandits' masks. One can say he stretches his synthetic face. One can say he reeks of disturbed graves. On nights like tonight—sultry like a Shirley Jackson story, gothic like a bleeding statue—Larry swears that in another life he was Maximilian II, son of the fabled Emperor of Mexico. Died from remaining unborn. Crying shame.

109. False Memory

Rough sketch of a false memory: "Ohmygod, it's Larry Rios, Chicano Poet Extraordinaire, Bad Boy Bard of Murder himself!" Nonplussed: "Howdy. Have we met?" "You've always known me. In the beginning was the Word, and the Word was with God, and the Word was me." "There she is. Who're your favorite poets?" "Probably Charles Rimbaud. Atticus. And duh, you, of course." "Attagirl, admirable Rimbaud—stopped publishing after his birth vicennial, that reprobate. But do you mean Arthur Rimbaud?" "Anyways. It's super awkward asking this, but, like, can you review my work sometime? I'll buy one of your books someday. I promise."

110. Parting Words

He devotes a weekend discerning the parting words he'd leave to his students on the final day of class—if he were a literature professor. What pressure. What philosophical encumbrance. Saturday morning, in the Starbucks drive-thru line, this is what he strings together: "And remember, dear students, all books are floating palaces, flying oases—you just gotta build your ladders high enough." Astoundingly corny. Maybe a tad too trite. Sunday afternoon, pumping gas, Larry Rios resettles on this: "And remember, dear students, all books are prisoners, wrongfully convicted—you just need to insert your cell keys, crank 'em all the way."

111a. Punchlines

In no symbolic order, a brief listing of punchlines to irreverent, idiotic jokes: "Mr. Borges, are you a fan of blind dates?" "Ms. Plath, you missed a spot in the oven." "Mr. Márquez, I mustache you about magical thinking." "Mr. Kafka, what're your plans on Father's Day?" "Mr. Hemingway, you're an exceptional marksman." "Mr. Kerouac, I said 'run,' not 'rum.'" "Ms. Woolf, you give horrible directions." I know, I know … terrible. Absolutely sophomoric. But also, kinda liberating. And a teeny bit thrilling. Larry Rios demands I make one correction; in the first sentence, where I put *idiotic*—change to *idiosyncratic*.

"Knock knock." "Who's there?" "I dunno who There is but that rapscallion's up to no good." "Ha." "Haha!" "HAHA." "HAHAHA." "Ha hee hoo." "Hoo ha hee." "So, whatchu listening to, goofball?" "'You Got Me' by The Roots featuring Erykah Badu. Been on repeat since 1999." "*I stepped off the stage and took a piece of her heart.* The dopest line." "The American Dream distilled." "Can't beat the Dream Team." "Red pill." "Rabbit hole." "Wonderland." "Everywhere you walk, symbols for justice or treachery. Death or liberty." "Ride or die." "Guns and roses." "Rinse and repeat." "You famished?" "Naw, but I can eat."

112. Writer Notes: Who's Who

Most suspiciously-read: all Americans. Startlingly approachable: Stephen King. Least approachable: you don't wanna know. Most guns in a briefcase: Oscar Zeta Acosta. Most monotone: Tao Lin. Most caffeinated: Balzac. Funniest surname (in the American tongue): Balzac. Brutally elegant: Toni Morrison. Brutally inelegant: Bukowski. Craziest: all of them. Filthiest: the list goes on. Applaudingly prolific: Joyce Carol Oates. Questionably prolific: taking the high road. Hippest: you wouldn't know them. Smartest in the room: none. Remarkably productive (yet low energy): they're a slow-moving target. Costliest ego: get in line. Criminally underrated: ?. Most poetic: ?. Goofiest mustache: Flaubert. Most bellybutton lint: Larry Rios.

113. Bandages

Food for thought: If you disappear Harry Houdini, you earn Loki's adoration for infinity. If you reinvent the wheel of passion, you pretzel romance poems into horror memoirs. If you cast the laws of brotherhood into fires of deconstruction, you marinate sentience in ponds of resurrection. If you read every book in the world but don't publish one, you're the Eyes of Big Brother: creaking shelf in the Library of Babel. If you're without pen or phone, scrape your verse into your palms. No supplies necessary for confession. Inside Larry Rios' medicine cabinet: boxes and boxes of bandages. Just in case.

114. Prophetess

He was a cub reporter when he met his inamorata, catching her eyes denoting a prophetess surveying rolling clouds and recognizing in them hallowed enigmas she cannot reveal to ordinary men. She was just a woman. Her right iris, brown, her left, hazel. Employed in a bookstore launched on the capital of a bankable author who croaked after grand opening, Lucia helped the newbie scoop scant inches of story. He returned to the newsroom with insignificant quotes, her phone number. He'd spoken more than he wished. Glitched. Anyone makes the smooth move in hindsight. She wore a plaid skirt, Popeye T-shirt.

115. Presumptuous

The story that made Larry Rios quit writing fiction: "Kolson," a metaphysical yarn narrated by a spaceman. The story begins: *Back when I was at the Academy, on the outskirts of the Red Asteroid Belt, I bunked for six months with a trainee whom I can still say, with absolute certainty, is the most remarkable person I've met.* Kolson is an eater of souls—a devourer of expired consciousnesses including Stan Lee's and Yuri Gagarin's (*who was betrayed by God*). What's juvenile about the piece, to Larry, is how he presumed to understand others (even in space) without first understanding himself.

116. Jack Nicholson's Face

The Shining. Jack Nicholson chatting with Lloyd the bartender. A ghost. Two ghosts, really. Spectral negotiations. Plastered on the screen: Jack Nicholson's wolfish grin. Arched eyebrows—fiendish, psychotic. Face of a burgeoning killer. Face of an imminent ax wielder. Shelley Duvall's equal—favored son. Rugged, riveting, renowned—America's face. Bargaining with no chips. Inventing rules. Commiserating ghouls. There's a story here, its pagan energy so authoritative it sends, for freeze-frame seconds, shivers up Larry Rios' spinal column. Horripilation. He will never write it. It's not for anybody else to write, either. This unprinted story of Jack Nicholson's face perishes with Larry.

117. Inexplicable Dream

Larry Rios' recent mulling over of parting words to make-believe students yields an inexplicable dream. (Ain't they all?) Inside the Concord School of Philosophy in—whoops, in a shack atop the Alamo—he runs the Chicano School of Gothic Noir, overseeing the education of snotnoses and whippersnappers, Skittles-complexioned and pioneering, malleable, all in coonskin caps. Two troublemakers engage in fisticuffs over a game of Uno. Headmaster Larry pinches their ears, assigns these kerfufflists a 101-page story. "Your novellas," he commands, "must contain unsolved murders, psychoactive cacti, Orbison's 'Only the Lonely' sung by an angel baby, and understated references to Porfirio Díaz."

118. Backroom Dream

One inexplicable dream ends, another immediately follows: "Howdy, ma'am. May you look up a book for me, please?" "Affirmative. Title, sir?" "It's an anthology, *The Chicano Anthology of Dream Poems and Latinx Unicorns*." "Hokay." Typing. Clicking. Click-clack-tap. "Drats. Machine's not pulling it. Who's the editor, sir?" "I'm one of the contributors. But I forgot to mention it's microscopic. Might I endorse calling upon your most penetrating microscope?" "Affirmative. Got it right here, sir. If I'm not back from the backroom in, say, three hours, call the president." "You're the bestest, ma'am." "What I have are a very particular set of skills."

119. Starship Captain

Another inexplicable dream ends, waking follows. Night's median. Slivers of moonlight slicing across blinds. Nights like this, he remembers, Lucia riding him like a crazed starship captain. Night like this, consecration—life ushered in, on a night like this. He remembers the evening she introduced him to *The Labyrinth of Solitude* by Octavio Paz, the man who tacked on whitey's map the agonized Mexican. You'll enjoy sampling his ideas, she said, seductive. And taste something rancid every page—bon appétite. Lucia's big family endowing her with a mouth larger than life. Overcrowdedness impelling her to blaze a trail of her own.

120. Another Dream

Asleep after indeterminate restlessness, no sooner's it a nothing-dream than he's entered a chandelier-lit passage-way—candlelights amplifying undeniable trepidation—into a hallway crammed with masks hung aslant on whitewall: African trickster masks, Japanese demon masks, Greek theater masks, Phantom of the Opera masks, King Tut masks, Richard Nixon masks, Nelson Mandela masks, Che Guevara masks, Margaret Thatcher masks, Batman masks, luchador masks, Jason hockey masks, Ghostface masks, spray-painted William Shatner masks, Guy Fawkes (and Fieri) masks, Dante Alighieri masks, Michael Jordan (and Jackson) masks, Pope JP2 masks, and, dead-end—a severed head. An intimate's. Our anguished dreamer all the while undressed.

121. Infinitesimal

Hard recovering a modicum of dignity after a rattling nightmare intended for deserting fathers and abandoned husbands rolled into one. The dawn sky, a caliginous yellow: a time machine. Atmospheric. Nostalgia chopping the bend of your knees. For we are p(r)awns—modest—infinitesimal—in the intergalactic frying pan stripping all to unintelligible singularity. Larry Rios puts on a finger-stained Etta James record—his mother's sound. Brushes his teeth longer than recommended. Doesn't shave. "Let thee grow," he says with contempt to the wraiths lingering outside his fugitive quietude. A bubble. The known world separated from indescribable cruelties rendered graciously unseen. Amen.

122. Questions

Questions for thought: Can the human filth that was Joseph Stalin be justified using a quadratic equation?—and Hitler, Schrödinger's equation? Can a one-page scroll bearing the world's most convoluted Irish novel (*Finnegans Wake*, to be sure) be fully stuffed inside a woman's purse (Kate Spade, preferably)? Can an unreliable poem (or reliable, for that matter) withstand the nitrogen-liquid surface of Titan, Saturn's largest moon? Can a reputedly scrupulous financier be trusted—truly trusted—to handle honorably the estate of a libertine duke? Can a poet's body of work outrace death, therefore achieving covetable immortality? A one-word answer to all: possibly.

123. Random Reviewers

Perusing the website Goodreads, Larry Rios reviews reviews of sorry-sack reviewers who reviewed masterpiece works including *Ulysses*, *Song of Solomon*, *Leaves of Grass*, *Posthumous Memoirs of Brás Cubas*, *Pale Fire* and *The Brothers Karamazov*. The contents of their commentaries can be summed up in the following locutions: *Interesting book. Well-written. Don't read it.* The "names" of reviewers include Chancie Phillips, Nunya_B, Carolina Weeper, LeLitWitch, ovidreader, Hermione Danger, Dick Diver, 50ShadesofPlayDoh, Chester Copperpot. Geniuses, Larry thinks. But it's Opposite Day. Would this disillusioned assembly recognize a *good* read if it slapped them upside the humerus? Would any of us, really? Really? Really?

124. Last Words

The old die young: The last words he's convinced he recalls escaping his grandfather's kisser just before expiration. Horse-riding accident. Broken ribs leaking soul beholden to body bound by time, that rigid shoe, contouring our foot, the supple soul—and what then if it's slipped off? Larry Rios remembers his grandfather's sandpaper hands death-gripping his wrists. The old die young. This he shared with Lucia during an overnight stay in a hospital due to sweltering fever. By his bedside, her startled reaction: Shut the fudging door, my gramps said the exact same thing, but he croaked a month after saying it.

125. Soreness

Munchausen's Syndrome: a psychological disorder where someone pretends to be ill or deliberately produces symptoms of illness in themselves. Something for everything these days. Lucia, he recollects, complained frequently of neck soreness. First subtle, then a trickling down of what she thought was tingling in her fingers, toes. Her very quintessence. Anything hurt? he'd asked. Headache? After applying a gel pack, she said (like clockwork), No, I'm sure it'll go away. You've been saying that, Luz. She downed an Ibuprofen, then said (like clockwork), It's nothing, hun, I feel perfect. Fine. Great. Forget it. Then: Not that you'd believe me anyway.

126. Brief Aside

Munchausen's Syndrome: named for the fictional eigh-teenth-century German nobleman Baron von Munchausen created by librarian/writer Rudolf Erich Raspe. Munchausen, in Raspe's 1785 novel, *Baron Munchausen's Narrative of his Marvellous Travels and Campaigns in Russia*, embellished life-signifying stories: riding/straddling a cannonball, battling a forty-foot crocodile, visiting the quicksilver moon. In 1988, director Terry Gilliam released *The Adventures of Baron Munchausen*, starring John Neville, Oliver Reed, Uma Thurman. It bombed financially but received critical admiration—factoids privy to a certain Larry Rios plugged into the information superhighway where hurtling lanes and no exits abound. Just watch the movie, you're thinking. And then what?

127. Limited Resource

Contrary to popular belief, empathy's a limited resource—physically and rationally. To be unlimitedly empathetic is to be a Swiss cheese wall—the air itself—no, dark matter, the stuff that is and is everywhere obscured from the faulty human eye. To be limitlessly empathic is to be God—New Testament God—unconditionally all-loving radiating all-encompassing love. "Magpies and fairytales," Larry Rios says aloud for no reason whatsoever (or so he assumes). (No reason whatsoever doesn't exist, like infinite empathy.) Out of cat's curiosity, Larry googles magpies, learns they're the only birds—the only nonmammals—known to achieve mirror self-recognition. Crafty.

128. Leaks

Some mornings, most mornings, many mornings, sunshine enters Larry Rios' body, then slowly, meekly—sadly—leaks out his fingertips, his bellybutton, his eyes. Not in the form of lasers or tears, but sorrow. A sorrow beyond tears. Natural event. Emotional humidity. Twitchy extremities. Make a sudden move and disappear. Today, he asks himself—half a chocolate Pop-Tart in mouth—"Amb bi a bell-abubed boed?" (Translation: "Am I a well-adjusted poet?") Scratches his left sideburn, the hairs there whitening rapidly. He allows his question to glide into realms undetected before answering himself: "BAHAHAHAHR-RRRRRK." (Translation: Pop-Tarts, contrary to popular belief, are easily provoked.)

129. Munchausen's Syndrome

Lucia had her neck soreness; he, his nightmare. She awoke one morning to an empty bed, found him on the living room rocker, under a blanket, shivering. What's wrong? she asked. Same ol' same ol', he answered. You're not catching a fever, are you? Not this time, he said. She went to the kitchen to fetch coffee, returned with two mugs in hand. After a little while, she asked, Was it her again? that snake chick? He sipped from his mug, the brew black as— Who else, he replied. Gazing down at her slippered feet, all she said back was, Okay.

130. Unnecessary Clarification

Forgiving reader, this is an unnecessary clarification, but when I mention that Larry Rios is a bibliophile, I mean platonically and romantically. As in, back when he dated Tina Sandiego, a former mime, they made love thrice (twice pantomimed) on the carpet within a circular arrangement of various editions of Hermann Hesse's *Siddhartha* witnessing meditatively Tina sink her nails in his back, scratch what felt like a fragmentary poem. She finished and whimpered, Je ne sais quoi. Books have been known to electrify Larry. A few, he isn't on speaking terms with. Others, he admires collegially, from afar, cordially, firmly friend-zoned.

131. Disrespect

Larry Rios, seated on the stairway outside his front door, smoking, observes a praying mantis perched on the iron handrail, motionless, staring seemingly into the Void with unkind insectile concentration. Thoughtlessly, Larry blows a noxious cloud at the mantis; it's unfazed, as if unconcerned, utterly bored, unthreatened. Larry snaps into reality (from his perspective), thinks, How rude, disrespecting this critter of streamlined majesty (that thorax, though!) from a species almost two-hundred million years old—I, from a race a measly—hey, that's my forearm. Ouch. Watch those tibial spines. I like your style, grasshopper. Your spunk. Keep showing 'em who's boss.

132. Unstoppable Fingers

When he first identified as a storyteller, he learned first-hand how writing affords its maker unparalleled unilateral control, the pen like Death's unstoppable fingers strumming ribcages to syncopations of daybreak, middlenight—songs—these machinations no less than sacrificial lambs disposed of at thought's speed, nerve signals traveling an expeditious 270 mph, disregarded much swifter, fates disgraceful as cumbersome coins however unlucky clanging in pockets nobody to begin with asked for—discordant—relegated to tip jars, prior sanctuaries to elements once spread across Wonder Bread, whose motive was always too transparent: keep pulses wondrously a-thumping, while willful hearts await their final reckoning.

133. 1982

Blade Runner is so 1982, Larry Rios thinks, watching the film. The brown brooding face of Edward James Olmos reminds Larry of his father. The prideful arrogance of a dark scowl. "Always cherish your queen," he remembers his dad advising in the chess-playing days—applicable guidance across the board. A verse from an OutKast song suddenly assaults him: *Thank God for Mom and Dad / For sticking two together / 'Cause we don't know how.* Always something. If not this, then that. Now's not the time to sink, Larry. Focus. *Blade Runner.* 1982. Coincidentally, the year of Philip K. Dick's death.

134. Lloyd the Bartender

Stop! Nobody told Larry Rios that Lloyd the bartender from *The Shining* is in *Blade Runner*. That ghastly actor, leapfrogging from one cult feature to another. And his 1982 glasses ... those unsightly goggles. His is a face that'll keep Larry up hours extra tonight. Lloyd the bartender—his real name: Joe Turkel. Born July 15, 1927, in Brooklyn. July 15, 1979—the date Philip K. Dick wrote a letter to Jonathan Ostrowsky-Lantz, then-editor of Unearth Magazine. July 15, 2016—the date an article was published online titled, "Reality is a bubble: The sci-fi of Philip K Dick, the fictionalising philosopher."

135. Synchronicity

"I guaran-damn-tee you they'll charge us for air next year," he hears one woman mansplain to another outside a café. Ah, thinks Larry Rios strolling by them, Dunning-Kruger effect—little fear goes a looong way in the hazy hours, in the midst of midsummer. She's probably right. He once considered self-publishing twenty-four chapbooks, each containing twenty-four poems for and during each hour of day (the twenty-four stars of the New Kingdom). But everybody knows that self-publishing's a kamikaze act, such an offense invalidating one's contributions indefinitely. Or he's got it all wrong. In those big-boy pants. Which makes everything come together.

136. Hard Times

"I've fallen on hard times. I'm a man of flesh and language. Soon my time'll be up. My words extinguished. I'm the sum of my words, Quetzalcōātl, a splinter off the ruler of sizzling suns and our blood moon—Christ's moon first. I'm a large-headed small mouth with delusions of grandeur, molehill provocations. A trombone begging for grease, soothsaying deceit, refusing transmutation. Man, I'm a man fallen on hard times. A fallen man, man. My love—my baby girl—maybe we'll meet again? And again. Again." This, a narcoleptic voice memo Larry Rios deletes not by accident. For the best. Amen.

137. Narcissus

Story goes that beautiful Narcissus knelt daily at a lake to marvel at his likeness, then one day fell in, drowned, the spot from which bloomed the daffodil, all variations containing the alkaloid poison lycorine, capable of killing when ingested, desired—directed. The poet as prophet, poet as deceiver, poet as Narcissus—assassin. When Larry Rios sees folks with long colorful fingernails—acrylic and oft-studded with rhinestones—he thinks, Back off, Narcissus, purveyor of vanity. He recalls Lucia had a habit of sometimes painting the nails of only one hand, leaving her others uncolored. It made her happy, is what matters.

138. Reformed Criminal

He skims a front-page article in today's paper. Jose Hayden—who'd been sentenced seven years for manslaughter, released early—is now, every weekend, baking cornbread for the city's impoverished. Larry Rios notices the words "Reformed criminal" in the headline, thinks, Ol' Joe, no matter how much reform you undergo—no matter how many pounds of maize you shove down the unquenchable throats of our collective goat-brains—the dispossessed—you'll always be, in their maws, a criminal. Reformed criminal. Once they brand you, here, you must manifest The Label's dastardly function. Such is the limitation, preoccupation, recrimination—damnation—of the English lengua.

139. Reevaluation

You can't capture beauty unless you murder it / Can't capture beauty lest you nurture it / So I invited Beauty to soak her in it / The hot Roman baths of lust(er). On a scale of one hundred, Larry Rios gives this poem's start a forty-two. An F, as in, "Eff this poem," which he takes out of this world with the pen that brought it into it. Do poets parent poems, or do poems locate willing surrogates? Overeager is another way of saying underprepared. Don't ever forget it, Larry. Beauty, good sir, never requires bathing. That one's for free.

140. Low-Key

When folks say they "low-key" want to believe in something, what they really mean to say is they "really" want to believe in something. It's a scorcher of a Friday midafternoon—his air conditioning blasting nonstop and the cicadas shrieking their insectile calls. He's got this itch all over. He's hydrated and ready to talk. Language remains a vehicle for communication. Language remains a vehicle for miscommunication. Language remains a vehicle for truth. Language remains a genre of deception—a hall of mirrors. Language isn't quite the slumlord she used to be for Larry Rios, but low-key, he anticipates eviction anytime.

141. Teeth

He witnesses the last ten seconds of life. Nothing changes, mostly. Such is the largesse of the cosmos—nothingness connecting nothingness, mostly. He rises, tastes metallic bitterness from REM sleep. Dead of night, flips open his blinds, considers the blurred horizon of his foresight. Stop me if you've heard this before: Man peers into stars, projects his grandeur, fears, onto boundless black spandex. Tonight, he's overcome—also relieved that, lately, she's kept distance. Because everything that's wrecked, she's to blame. Right? Regardless, man must bite back his demon. Larry Rios' teeth: intact, resilient. Twenty-eight genetic gifts. Ah. How fast everything changes.

142. Visitor

Thursday evening. Knock on the door. Through the peep-hole, there he was. How may I assist you, officer? Ven. Nelson—sandaled, cargo shorted, emanating an uncertain expression—stepped inside and straightaway handed him a paper sliver. You'd think it was the Holy Grail in his possession, reading on the note a hastily scribbled number in red ink. If anyone finds out, Nelson said. Nelly, we're good in the hood, baby. Tip-top. How 'bout a drink? I thought you didn't vibe with the imbibe? Correctamundo—I don't. Nuts, I should be investigating you, but— Folgers, milk? Rat poison, he chose, partway joshing.

143. Directive

He knew not to ask him too many questions about the war. He wasn't a violent man, his father, but you never really could predict when the temperature would flip. One glimpse at his reddened scleras and you could smell the blood-soaked jungles—enlarged veins like the Congo River in Conrad's *Heart of Darkness* snaking into his barsoap brain a savage, entangled, unforgettable history. While playing chess one day, the clouds swollen a tempestuous blue-green, his father told him, Boy, you're gonna spend the summer with your grandpa. In Mexico. At which point he checkmated the child. Rain poured. Jesus wept.

144. Second Funeral

He didn't want to hear his son's protests, but out of respect handed him a ragged hardback on the chronicles of Mexico purchased at a garage sale whose organizer has returned to dust. Larry Rios recalls his father asking him to fetch the old straw hat in the closet. He threw the hat in the fireplace, squirted onto it lighter fluid, then asked him to retrieve from the pantry jumbo marshmallows, soon roasted over the burning hat. Papa, that belong to a dead solider? An old friend, said the father. They chewed solemnly their charred treats. The child's second funeral.

145. Strange Fruit

Buddy Holly's "Everyday" plays on Pandora. Holly the sound of his father, Etta James his mother. Forever and ever. Amen. Then there's Billie Holiday's "Strange Fruit." *Blood on the leaves and blood at the root.* His life a strange fruit in a strange garden. Fruit doesn't fall far from the root. Somewhere inside, Lucia's voice. Mist. Why were you kneeling over the baby last night? Slowly they danced, stepped side to side. Were you whispering a prayer in her ear? He answered: I told her I'll always be her father. That I'll protect her forever and ever. (Forever: an immortal's trade.)

146. Suggestive

Larry Rios searches for the volta to his suggestive sonnet, chews off his thumbnail, spits it out in the bathroom, looks mirrorward, asks: "So *what*?" That shiny chemical concoction making mincemeat of otherwise routine pitstops. "I asked you a question you two-faced lede-burying mother-fudger." Larry shrugs; his reflection mimics. Later, in an unspecified coffeehouse, Eartha Kitt's XXX(mas)-rated "Santa Baby" (it's the most wonderful time of the year) rides the airwaves—sign, gift, cream whipped from thin air, unlocking force: *No—my lust was always stuffed up the chimney.* "Naughty," whispers he, alone with himself, thus unalone, jotting away, compassion incarnate. "Nice."

147. First Kill

It was December 3, 1967. A forward operating base near Hue. At exactly 0400 hours he snuck out about a quarter-klick south of camp to take a whiz in solitude. Five minutes and one gunshot later he cradled the corpse of a fighter—a young woman. He clipped two long strands of her black hair, attached them with drying mud to the sides of his rifle. In the warm breeze they rustled like bicycle streamers. He wrote poems about her, for her, in her voice—called them psalms. Gave them to a buddy who, discreetly, incinerated the scribblings with his Zippo.

148. Penny-Wisdom

Sycophants and succotash—connection? Lord knows, but on another note, how'd the jingle go, back when No. 45 was a fake TV celebrity? *Money money money money, money.* "For The Love of Money" by The O'Jays, 1973, the year Tricky Dick begunneth his second presidential term. Watergate, waterboarding; the former transpired in 1972, the latter during the Genesis flood, when the straw that broke Noah's back was twin parrots nagging him to pray-pray before bed. Examining a one-dollar bill and a Benji, Larry Rios notices that both Founders' lips are condescendingly pursed, as if to suggest, "A penny saved ain't shit."

149. Fractures

Larry Rios logs into his New York Times account, watches a compilation of nationwide protests-turned-riots. Manic camerawork, guttural wails for medics, for mom. God's imagined creatures. Human condition. City life. A work in progress. (Progressive erosion?) A youthful man is interviewed. He wears Malcolm X browline glasses, dreadlocks. Turns his head to display a battle wound on his cheek stamped by a trooper's teargas canister. "I didn't ask for this," he says, his scar yet unsealed, "but this, for reform, is always what it takes." A chopped sentence in fractures, sutured, butchered in full. To true strangers, never saying, Hey, stranger.

150. Midpoint

Darling reader, this page isn't my playground. This sandbox is publicly owned. Characters herein aren't puppets molded to my slippery wiles. This isn't a massively multiplayer online role-playing game. Here—each of us flailing into animation as couriers strapped with time-bombs, trekking terrains outward, inward, emulating Nature's ire, innocence, until there we're returned—here, this place called home. Enough waxing. There was a writer who killed so many folks in his stories he got the idea to try it himself. He discovered life's cheap, changed his name outta cowardice, stopped attempting fiction. Kept a low profile (kinda). With me so far?

The Snake-Haired Lady

151. Passing

Larry Rios' least favorite coworker in a rare showcase of solidarity asks him while passing him in the hallway, "Read any good books lately?" Larry answers snippily, "Not enough," defaulting to broad-stroke malaise. He wonders in the span of a dozen brisk steps, Do the stars possess consciousness in the hour of their demise? Do celestial bodies pray for others in the hour of the star? He can't determine in this moment why these questions preoccupy him. Fact is, they strike him as prescient, pearlescent. "Good luck with that," his coworker leaves him with. His mouth clamps shut—a closed book.

152. Backwards

He reads a newly arrived email from *MAGA: Make America Gyrate Again—The Literary Magazine for Witches, Warlocks and Them-Bots from the Briar Patch*. "Dearest Yrral Soir, thanks a trillion for your submission. We'd enjoy placing a publishing spell on 'Yuka wuka' and 'Yuka suka mutha-truka' if the poems remain available." He spots a postscript below the acceptance message: "P.S. Is Yrral Soir your nom de plume? We mean no offense. We correspond peaceful-ly. Our sorcerous staff does request that you disclose your Christian name, lest you desire a hellacious curse—incurable garlic breath, some such. Okeydokey?" "ll'I kniht tuoba ti."

153. Proposal

In "N.Y. State of Mind," Nas asserts *sleep is the cousin of death*. With sleep also the mother of life, an evolved question's begged: Are life and death second cousins? Anyhow, here's the story of the last time Larry Rios genuinely asked for help. After a particularly charged class, he swung by Professor Maximillian Masterson's office. A minutest minute of your time, sire? The philosopher peeled away his well-traveled eyes from a rashly constructed essay. Son: your thirteenth MLA citation's hogwash. Second: you misspelled Nietzsche, doggonit. Counterstriking: And you mispronounced Wittgenstein—sire. Smirking: Audacious whippersnapper. Whatever it is, answer's yes. Siéntate.

154. Performance

Larry Rios pays for a gallon of 2% milk and Andy Capp's Hot Fries, ponders the elusive meaning of the phrase *moral imperative*, when the cashier unpromptedly clues him in on some hysterical woman. "She was drunkern a monkey in a moonshine barrel. Back at my other store." "Bliss is ignorance," Larry quick-wittedly. Outside the gas station a homeless-seeming one-armed man solicits Larry. "Do you take Discover?" Larry quick-wittedly. "I can play the trumpet," the other counteroffers. Larry deliberates. "Free sample?" Minus a trumpet, the performance is impassioned. "One arm, too," Larry esteems. "Chin-ups're quite difficult." The free trial has ended.

155. Second Visit

He opened his door, surprised to see him again. Well I'll be tickled, my favorite civil servant. Welcome to my wasp factory! The off-duty officer slipped inside. Before cutting to it, nervous delay, he pointed at his pocketed hands, requested, Let's remove our hands from our pockets, yeah? He complied, replied: Time's a precious thing, never waste it, à la Willy Wonka. Nelson: Speaking as a buddy here, but I called your ex—had to. Procedurally: Give me your version what happened. He, already barreled into the past, scanned Nelson's waist—ungunned. Cigarette? I thought you quit. You ain't far off.

156. Supper

Larry Rios bites into a Nacho Cheese Doritos Locos Taco, moans. Proof he's trapped under free enterprise's thumb more than he cares to believe. Processed chihuahua meat, shredded cheese shoved into cardboard sarcophagi, sour cream shot out of patented Taco Bell® guns—acid pulverizing intestines, producing for some excruciating orgasms. Mother Nature, Daddy Greenbacks; Larry: mere byproduct of their toxic union. Backwash in the receptacle of civilization. You are what you eat. Moan now, cry later. Deep breaths. Stomach the brunt of free will's repercussions. Let it out. I was right about you, though I won't throw it in your two-face.

157. Invisible Parties

Italo Calvino was the kind of writer who erected forbidden cities in barren mental landscapes, witnessed the birth of micro-galaxies in the aftermath of two blades of lawn grass brushing against one another. Vultures, to Calvino, were the beating hearts of prune-sized fetuses: messengers from Innana, Mesopotamian fertility goddess. Larry Rios suddenly envisions what his Italian mancrush would've done had he bumped into Lucia at a soiree. Calvino, slick postmodernist, would've gawked at her different-colored eyes, published two experimental novels vehemently opposed yet romantically chained. Flattered, Lucia would've hated them. Dreamed about him. "A good writer's a dead writer," Larry jealously.

158. Portrait

He never knew his paternal grandmother, all evidence of her compressed in a portrait—unsmiling newlyweds inexperienced yet impossibly aged. His grandfather claimed she was from a Sicilian village where Mussolini himself, it was said, tossed the strangled bodies of dissidents into the Mediterranean Sea. The photograph hung across his grandfather's dining table, meals accented by her stony glare. War's been rough on your papa, his grandfather said. Grandpa, said the boy, how'd Grandma die? Too much smoking, answered the old man, glancing at the photo. Was she a nice lady? He sipped his cerveza, sighed, said, Go outside, mijito. Play.

159. Condition

Her condition was that he not write stories based on the reality of their baby, that their daughter's story was sacred and should remain unbruised from the handcuffs of the fantastical. She felt this way too about their arguments but understood that demanding him to also refrain from assembling material from their marital activities would've been like telling a circus tiger to not view his master as soft-skinned snack. He acquiesced, but pointed out that babies' realities, unsurprisingly, are identical, and that as precious as their beautiful Comet was, she was statistically unremarkable in that regard. Lucia, flustered, pinched his buttcheek.

160. Comet

On his knees, polo dampened, Levi's dirtied, hair disheveled, he wrapped his arms around her waist, pressed his ear into her swollen abdomen. Flush of gastric juices. She caressed his head as he told her about the burnt bodies, noble firemen, apathetic policemen. A cruel summer night's trappings, meanwhile summoning deadlined words for the ravenous readership—diminishing subscribers. Another sidebar throwaway. How must one begin again? Lucia saw something flash across the sky, a brilliant green stroke. A sign. A silver lining against innumerable perils above and beyond. And she said, Comet. We'll name the baby Comet, is what she said.

161. Come Again

Remember when Larry Rios went to the gas station, encountered a phantom-trumpet-playing one-armed homeless musician? Okay, different day, same culprit, except this time, after the vagrant solicits Larry again—declining from him a lamentable nickel—dude puts on another knockabout performance, but instead of with a phantom trumpet, an air guitar. He shreds: the best Larry's ever heard. "Did your trumpet grow legs?" Larry's curious to know. "I play everything. I'm a bad man. Gimme a song. Just none of that Nickelback." "What's your band's name?" "Come Again." "Your stage name?" "Come Again." "Come again?" "That's it." "Come Again?" "You dumb?"

162. Meticulous

Larry Rios writes a poem about Yuks the sword-swallow-ing frog combating, on unicycle, a bear clad in Roman legionnaire armor. Yuks unsheathes his sword from his sore throat, pokes the bear's exposed kneecaps; the bear thrusts his spear at Yuks, fantasizing how the defiant amphibian will taste. Larry—professional daydreamer—deliberates every word, these atomically charged stand-ins for images that are stand-ins for a mélange, a farrago, of meaning that's a stand-in for another tattoo on the old brain folds. There're kiddy tattoos, then there's laser removal. The poet as meticulous tattoo artist. (Are words our only agency of control? Possibly.)

163. Soundbite

"If Jane Austen had written a pastiche on sassy gargoyles."
This shrapnel of bookstore dialogue strikes ambling Larry
Rios as just the thing a bookseller might say to a cohort.
It *is* just the thing she'd said—ingénues, the lot of them.
Hey, cool it, Larry. The ombré-maned and pastel-brained
do bite back. Don't gotta be rich and famous to say whatever you please. To be (or not to be) somewhere crammed
with flamboyant banality. Banal—sinister-sounding but
with an innocent definition. See also: benign. As in: Your
tumor's benign. Larry's buzz is killed. Buzzkill—a word
through which nobody dies.

164. Aficionado

Larry Rios—no-prize poet extraordinaire—loves the magnetism of couplets—microcosms of the dichotomous soul. But he adores more the stamp of triplets—holy triumvirate of some's lord and savior. However, his allotment of agnosticism aside, Larry venerates sinfully those panoramic quatrains—preferred method of discourse by the happiest man to breaststroke our planet of lost cultures, Nostradamus. On overcast days of European proportion, Larry's incapable, unequivocally unable, to ignore sonnets' fetching shadows—Shakespeare's sex appeal condensed, ziplocked in iambic pentameter. Concubine of rhyme, mastermind of beautify, aficionado of epics—ladies and gents: you're smitten, or you're not reading hard enough.

165. Culture Shock

Back in Larry Rios' undergrad days, when men were still not men and bejeweled blue jeans tried genially to balm Sunday scaries, his foremost brush with outside culture occurred on the campus rec center hardwood where a six-foot-something wispily mustached phenom the kids called ABCD went up for a finger roll. Undersized Larry—before he was Larry—leapt to contest this alphabetical colossus whose knee slammed into his opponent's manhood but not before an unclipped fingernail clipped the rock crucial degrees westbound for what benchwarmers misremembered as a superman stuff. Goliath saluted our writhing rim protector. Smack talk took a walk.

166. Fishline

It wasn't getting racked on a basketball court by a swaggering Indian or the exponentially weighty after-class chats with Professor Masterson that taught Larry Rios the world's tinier, vaster than he'd pretended—not to mention that scary summer in timeworn Mexico with his seemingly grief-proof widower grandfather who'd arrive at the end of his tunnel with a horrorstruck expression on his death mask—but hour by hour our pro-agonist snuggled into his pelt, improved his discernment of the ever-present near-invisible thread, the flimsy fishline, on which we traipse, scarcely addressing, prudently—having experienced one's life as only oneself, thus spoke Nietzsche.

167. Bite

Her second visit she poured warm poison inside his body, her hair roving, tongue hissing over his thigh. She bit down hard. In the morning his grandfather inspected the red puncture, said, A harmless little spider bite, mijito. Be tough. God punishes crybabies. The boy straightened his back, rubbed his stinging lesion, accepted a sip of his grandfather's cerveza, fulfilling the family custom into manhood. Having suppressed the pain a second time, and after refusing a smoke, reminding Grandpa that he was only a kid, he was sent outside where he baked and tanned under that mad lantern the Mexican sun.

168. Irreality

Larry Rios shifts into reverse—presumedly—extends his right arm behind the passenger headrest, cranes his head toward the back window, watches for traffic, anticipating rearwards motion. But his glossy pollution box remains stationary as an emerald. The irreality of the mundane faux pas spawns a transitory sense of displacement causing double vision and Larry's throat to dispense a "woo woo woo!" à la Curly from The Three Stooges. Irreality— where'd I last hear that gem? stalling Larry ruminates. The gym with the paraplegic attorney? Locker-room talk of legal quagmires? Lawyers're blockheads. (But as with real doctors, you want stellar ones.)

169. Strike One

After getting her number (digits, he'd called them), after phoning three days later, after taking Lucia out on a date, then two more, arriving at the impasse where the woman with the brown right iris, the hazel left, had a decision to make—dismantle her defenses, let his words invade; or escape—after she swung for the latter, not understanding why at the time, the rookie reporter remembered his father's advice—save a piece of yourself for you. Weeks later, our heartbroken antihero, covering a clown convention, met former mime Tina Sandiego. Days later, he was sweet-talking into her good ear.

170. Odd Couple

As recounted earlier, the odd couple made whoopee thrice within an arrangement of various editions of *Siddhartha*. Tina Sandiego introduced our correspondent to the venerable French poets: Baudelaire, Verlaine, André Breton (whom Larry Rios later learned was thrice married, eliciting from him an "Attaboy"). She was always clipping something: coupons, bangs, toenails. She lectured her beau on the benefits of environmental stewardship. Showered once weekly, turned her underwear inside out. Svelte, inquiring, high-strung, she was the first woman to whom he'd read his stories. She listened, with one good ear, better than anyone. Her spell: disappearing Lucia—or so it felt.

171. Bumper Sticker

About irreality: If it didn't happen, but you have your voice, then shout! On the congested freeway Larry Rios spots ahead of him a bumper sticker: *My dachshund's smarter than your honor student.* Unlikely. A scene from yesteryears floods him—Comet waddling into their bedroom, diaper wrapped around her curlyhead, a substance smeared around her mouth he hoped to Saint Pete was pudding. He sniffed: yep, pudding. Filthy animal, he said spiritedly. Her retort: Poopoo lips! Girl ain't right. Must be the Emily Dickinson before bedtime. Electronicless diversions, those years. Daddy, what's a real man? Where to begin. Where to end.

172. Muddy Greens

Later, when he asked what compelled her to say yes, she answered, Your eyes, deep-sea fisherman of compliments. To which he responded: Gracias, Ma. She beamed, couldn't understand he was actually thanking the imperceptible entity known as his biological mother. Indeed, his muddy green eyes, like clovers surrounding a campfire, won him a wife. A distracting color he'd inherited from Mom, who, with southerly grace, dallied into an early grave. He'd never addressed her as Mom. Just Ma. Gone so long like a pasture razed to nonexistence by the overlord called time having had its pitiless way. There are worse fates.

173. Tomorrow, Today

Uncle John, last he ever saw him, was doing knuckle pushups inside his efficiency apartment, cramped like everything around him, a struggle maintaining a physique ravaged by ex-ball and chains and health scares, incalculable mortality carved into him. Not much longer, he updated his nephew, who wanted to say, You need to be held, but settled for, You need a friend. What good're friends, neph, if members of our tribe clock out after— Shuddup, tío, you could suit up for the Oilers tomorrow no problemo. Later, he wondered night and day, Why say *tomorrow* instead of *today* to Ma's only brother?

174. Irreparable

You're being irrational, Lucia said to him upon his refusal to entertain the notion of scheduling an appointment with a shrink to discuss The Snake-Haired Lady, the egregiously recurring episodes packaged as demons from a mostly sheltered past that never vacated his headspace, like slothful squatters, selfish parasites—childhood stories omnipresent and permanently game to suit up anyplace, anytime. Writing exercises. Irrational, he repeated, his tone indicating, she knew, his typical deflection of matters paramount to her. He was being a troll. You're a rash and I'll, he said, leaving incomplete the skewed, absurd clause. Some rhymes, unsensible. Some tribulations: irreparable.

175. Lovely Night

Tonight's a night for wanderlust within local confines—inhaling the city's generational insulation. Popped-collar exuberance. Ogles from strangers. Curbside jazz. Ears wide open. Filet mignon. Chocolate mousse smeared on the pages of your favorite versifier. (As John Adams axiomatically said, you're never alone with a poet in your pocket.) Tonight's a night for wooing the moon. Entrancement. What to wear? Cardigan? Leather jacket? Larry Rios holds both in front of the fishbowl. "Bruce Lee, pick." The freethinking betta darts toward the jacket. Taking after its master. "Exquisite taste," Larry praises. "Be water, my friend," says she zero leagues under the sea.

176. The Pack

You'd've thought his accusation was a curse, but there's no classy way to tell somebody he's a miserable death-loving old zombie. His grandfather booted him outside, and in the distance a pale figure paced down a knoll, raising swirls of dirt, and through the swirls several heads emerged—a gang of boys tailing him, each one flinging rocks at him downhill. As they moved closer, he noticed some of them barefoot, some shirtless, all of them blowing chalky smoke. He heard them jeering at their target, Idiota. He puffed his first cigarette that day. Observed the pack stone the sullen-faced mute.

177. Disclosure

The professor yawned; after his mouth shut but before his face reset, his eyes disclosed severity the student'd witnessed on his father. Intently: You serve in 'Nam? Professor Masterson removed his glasses, rubbed his temples, sipped whiskey. I'm preposterously ancient. Intriguedly: Pops did a tour there—he'd've done Korea, too, age not restricting. Professor Masterson frowned. I was outta the service by then. PTSD's a moral injury. Morale injury, too, thought his student. His crow's feet crept past his face's edges. Naively: Didn't Wittgenstein say the self's strictly a linguistic problem? Son—your source on page thirteen ain't peer-reviewed. Replace it.

178. Half-Satisfied

Larry Rios leaves half a slice of astonishingly greasy pizza uneaten, considers writing a scathing Yelp review, remembers Yelp's an infestation, then carouses a DVD Exchange, buys a battleworn copy of *Face/Off*, watches it, snickers at Nic Cage's forceful performance, woolgathers about a ska band called Forceful Performances, snickers, craves a Snickers bar, heads to the john, grabs a pair of grooming scissors and, with the resolve of a seasoned surgeon, gently traces his face's outline in the mirror, says aloud—to himself—to lingering phantoms—"Perhaps my face is one-sided," then places a call, hangs up, heads to beddy-bye. Drools

179. Mother's Day

While she washed dishes he snuck into their room, took an envelope, spent the evening writing lines on it. Next morning, Mother's Day, he gifted her his poem. Clichéd, a child's work, still she kissed the paper, his forehead, hugged him and thought about the yellowed wads stuffed in her husband's toolbox—odes to a foreign rebel, the slain body, gunshots, LBJ, the dead girl's ascent to the otherworld. Holding it together, she told her son: Write a story for me too, sweetie. Go write me a nice story and I'll bake you some cookies. Sweet, delicious chocolate chip cookies. Mmm.

180. Disproportionate

Disciplines aside, the difference between Maximillian Masterson and Sola Dupré was the latter's willingness to extract a glimmer of funny in the valleys of despair throughout lectures. Her eyes optimistic, teeth large and shining, Professor Dupré, whose Creole ancestry, she'd claimed, was a source of measureless pride and shame, was an educator first, a poet second, finding in academia an employer funding dual passions. Larry Rios—before he was Larry—received a B in Professor Dupré's Intro to Poetry course. He'd written one masterly poem in class, which prevented him from earning the C the remainder of his sloppy work deserved.

181. Tough Crowd

After prolonged deliberation, Larry Rios returns to the gas station with the one-armed "multi-instrumentalist" and next to said gentleman sets down on the curb a sheet of paper folded long-ways that says *Chicano Poet Extraordinaire* front-facing. Larry reads fresh poetry aloud to comers, goers, and unlike the time he pulled this stunt at the Alamo, he's received coldly. Come Again abandons post, bedraggled, majorly ticked. An oyster-haired woman in cowgirl boots, humongous sunglasses, says to Larry, "Yoohoo." "Pardon?" "Yoohoo." "Ma'am?" "You who!" "Me Larry?" She tips him two nickels. "One for your pahtner." "Oh, see, he's got this vendetta against nickels."

182. Folks-Pleaser

Nelson, he said, I tell you about the time I studied under the poet Sola Dupré? More like farted around in perpetuity. She was gorgeous, kinda mummyish, a teaspoon of black widow. She was a disciple of Robert Hayden, and supposedly a cousin of James Weldon Johnson. I did horribly in her class, hadn't peeped inside yet to find poetry peeping back. She told me nobody'd ever flunked her course, that I'd be the first to make history. Would my ancestors be proud? They wouldn't recognize me from a Pterodactylus. Then I realized I had to kill the folks-pleaser in me.

183. Spooky

Thus, chewing on it later—presently—what make Maximillian Masterson and Sola Dupré, disciplines aside, one in the same (possibly oblique) for Larry Rios were their sheer (possibly oblivious) capacities to outmaneuver the laws of aging. Because James Weldon Johnson entered eternal rest in 1938, which would've meant Professor Dupré … "spooky," Larry spookily, holding in his mitts a hot-off-the-press edition of *MAGA: Make America Gyrate Again—The Literary Magazine for Witches, Warlocks and Them-Bots from the Briar Patch*, in which two of his poems are unleashed. Glee and hubris—kissing cousins—compel Larry to autograph, in Sharpie, his author copy.

184. John Hancocks

Here's a freaky one for you, frisky reader. Larry Rios gets home from work, supercharged, kicks off his Chucks—gradually browning like autumnal leaves—and, carrying heapings of sickly-sweet deficiency, sprinklings of longing, a dash of remorse, insubstantiality, retrieves from his bookshelf a signed copy of José Saramago's *Blindness*—it'd cost him a blinding amount of income—and his self-signed copy of *MAGA*, then, facing the signatures toward each other, rubs together both John Hancocks. Ah, tender buttons. Chafing pages whose qualities are, frankly, defiantly unalike. Larry's lascivious bones, chaos-prone, ache like a Marvin Gaye song. Too dead inside to cry.

185. Fruit Salad

He'd put her feet in her shoes *for* her, tie the laces tight if applicable. Floss her teeth, extracting therapeutic sighs. Brush her hair post-showers, remove clumps from bristles. Spoon-feed her cereal, soup. Peel off her Hot Pilates-swampy socks. Snatch boogers cliffhanging from her nose, which she detested—before a surge of impermanency toward her eccentric man flipped her back around. (Occasionally, still, she refused this nasal beautification.) This, his game of love. You make me feel like an invalid, Lucia said. Who you callin' a fruit salad? Picking fights giving rise to epicurean feasts o'er their king-size mattress game board.

186. Grand Larceny?

They left the bar, ringing ears caused by an indecisive playlist's rockabilly and rap. He'd unloaded major-league baggage; Professor Masterson sunk himself in Johnnie Walker. He gripped the professor's keys talismanically as they neared his vehicle. Professor M. eyed the unoccupied truck parked beside his. Suppose it's locked? He tested it, opening the driver's door, unimpressed, slamming it shut. Why lock our property? Keep thieves out? proposed the acolyte. Keep honest folk honest, corrected the master, burping vaingloriously. After-hours lesson, grasshopper. On the house. (And for all his erudition? Alcohol's victim. Like a gilded desperation. What cannot be said, be unsaid.)

187. Goodwill

Larry Rios, youalreadyknow extraordinaire, wraps up Jeet Kun Do training via YouTube. He's wiped, exhausted, pooped, drained. He thinks about his recent shenanigan at the gas station, reading untested work to uninterested patrons, triggering the "musician" Come Again to leave his spot, costing him, perhaps, a day's wages. "Do right—compensate, grasshopper," Larry instructs himself, returning to the gas station, unhurriedly approaching Come Again, who registers Larry frostily. Larry says, "I arrive goodwillingly," hands Come Again twenty bucks, asks earnestly, "What's your real name?" "This shit again." "Come Again?" "That's my name, knucklehead, don't wear it out." Insult taken in stride.

188. Toolbox

Nelson, he said, I tell you about the time my pops whooped the stuffing outta me? Really let me have it? It was after I got back from Mexico and had nightmares about rotting dark horses. Well, I'm dribbling the basketball outside, right? And the rock bounces inside the garage, bangs his toolbox and dents the side of it. My dad was mostly docile, but he flew into a rage. He didn't like nobody messing with his toolbox. My mom restrained him in a headlock. I think he wanted to kill me. And now, they're all gone. I'm fresh outta ancestors.

189. Tense

Reclined on his sofa, Larry Rios feels the pinch of a back muscle. Stoops over. A dog barks outside twice. Larry's stomach growls, complains—he'd skipped breakfast—thus the headache trickling across his dome. "When the mouth stops yakking, leave it to your meat suit to fill in the negative spaces," he says grandiloquently, scanning his screwy-smelling pantry: Jif Extra Crunchy peanut butter, expired package of Chips Ahoy!, Del Monte canned peas, pita chips, wheat bread. Larry fancies himself as shoddy mechanics, amateur improvisation, unwatchable film in an empty theater—yet he still has the eerie sense he's being severely analyzed.

190. Clamped

Nelson, he said, I tell you about the time I tried ending it with my ex-chica, former mime Tina Sandiego? Had my sights set on another—my future ex-wife—and ol' Sandiego sniffed it. She clamped down hard. Gary Payton Glove-level defense. She said, You're the only joker I want in my deck—the ozone opened and handed you to me—I love you with all my chi. La vache. Shush—my plasma pumps like drums, papi. Mime, you said? Nelson said. Correctamundo—puertorriqueña. And this was, attempted breakup? Consider your consciousness expanded—de nada. Welp, your ancestors would be proud.

191. Final Warning

Nelson—whose week involved a burning condominium and a pregnant teenager overdosed on painkillers—wanted to tell his sorry friend that he needed to see a therapist. Instead, he commiserated with him about progeny's absence. We miscarried last year, Nelson shared. He said to the cop, Man, didn't know y'all'd lost a kiddo. Nelson clicked his tongue. You never asked. As he left, and with the presumption in mind that cops snagged bad guys not through steadfast diligence but rather providential dice rolls, he issued him a warning. Don't ever come back here unannounced. Revenge: a dish best served to equals.

192. Lost Pages

For an absentee daddy, Larry Rios is a funny guy in the tragicomic sense of a man who's gained the world but has lost the pages of his one and only autobiography. Contrarian, irritable, soaring blood pressure and irrepressible fatalism instigated by intelligence bordering aimlessness. Let's drop the pretense. Larry'll never know that his daughter, in this moment containing all time, weeps in the arms of some maternal relative, seeking consolation for the bullying remarks her classmates spewed about her differently colored eyes—motherly, unreturnable gifts. Each sunrise, Comet's father: a non-entity buried deeper in the psychic wasteland of no return.

193. Probed

After class one day Professor Dupré advised him to swing by her office. Instantaneously he noticed a banker's lamp illuminating a human skull, upon which burned a black candle. Asked to whom the skull belonged, she replied, nonchalantly, her great-great-grandfather Claudius, of Mamluk descent. She motioned him to sit and, with fingers laced, probed about his future. Have you contemplated your education beyond graduation? He shrugged. Your poem, she said, captivated me. He left flattered yet unable to shake the macabre visage of splattered candle-wax on the ancestral cranium. She'd failed to inform it was a replica. Guiltily amused was she.

194a. Regular

Larry Rios skim-reads a New York Times book review in which the reviewer complains for half his article about the famously reclusive author's reclusivity instead of reviewing his slim late-career novel. The reviewer calls this particular job a *plum assignment*. Plum-brained snob, Larry critiques. He swings by Starbucks, orders the same ol'—grande Italian roast—notices on the barista's fleshy bicep a tattoo of a hamsa atop a pyramid. "Enjoy, Mr. Rios," fuchsia-haired Tamerina says. He cringes, responds, "I'm a regular now, aren't I?" "We're all regulars somewhere," says Tam, her declarative sounding to Larry like a b-sides Rolling Stones song.

194b. Service

(If Larry Rios chews on it—he does and doesn't—book reviews are in service to publishing houses in service to centers of commerce in service to consumers in service to taxes in service to the IRS in service to the gubmint in service to law imposed by law enforcement in service to the public good comprised of a perplexingly imbalanced public ill-defined by data points which're moving targets—an aggressive figure of speech, which is Western philosophy—one among Death's multivarious love languages. Yikes. What's more American than apple pie? Lies. Disguises. Marketing. Pools. Buying makes a cool kid cool.)

195. Write On

In a so-called turn of mundanity, a text from an unfamiliar number arrives. Hey. Too vague for specificity, too casual for incidental. Nelson, surely—right? All possibilities are numbing and in the age of digital distraction and technological tangle, Larry Rios—whose mind is shot 90% of waking hours—writes on, unaccompanied. For he's a jolly good poet, and abnormal texts cannot halt our anomalous associate's artistic advancement. "I'll deal with you shortly, holmes," he threatens his mobile. His new poem's title: "We're all regulars somewhere." It'll never see publication. Not for lack of trying. The post-Eden world a forlorn hope.

196. Accident

During a weekend hike, Comet a toddler, Lucia sprained her ankle. Driving her to the clinic, he swerved to avoid a darting deer, crashed into a tree, Lucia's head banging against the dashboard. Their car: drivable. He held it together. From his in-laws' house he taxied with Comet to the hospital, bit his hand to stifle tears. Recovering, Lucia contracted pneumonia. Their daughter dazed for months, his blood pressure skyrocketing. Not once throughout this trial did The Snake-Haired Lady visit him. Comet would always vaguely recall her father's desperate embrace, immense. Daddy, are the white chess pieces heroes or villains? Correctamundo.

197. Oranges

And so, the Giant Orange Peel occupied the Oval Office, his presence so invasive, so blistering, luck-drenched, it couldn't be ignored, though we've tried, patient reader. Such is historical protocol. Reflex. (Reflux?) For all of its lofty aspirations, all writing is factionist, spawned from that prefrontal cortex placemat from which we are one—and blindspotted. Science patronizing mystery. Pfft. If Larry Rios were a literature professor—thank Yahweh he isn't—he'd refuse invitation (for justifications sensible only to yo' mama) to sit on his university's diversity council, compromising tenure track, more—"you're fired" stinging, theoretically, like cheap salsa one buys anywhere.

198. Confession

Past closing, they parked under a palm tree at Dairy Queen, made hasty love, bodies enwrapped in a day's oily sheen. Afterwards, as lovelorn men are wont to do, he dropped knowledge on her, a verbose confession she swallowed whole. She grabbed from her purse a polaroid camera, snapped his shadowed semblance against the moonlight. Why'd you do that? he asked Tina Sandiego. Because liberty, equality, fraternity. Because no man's been as candid with me. Honestly, this pic's proof you're real. He loved her for that. Stroked her nipple. My body, given for you. Her pulsating heart pantomimed in her hands.

199. Cedar Fever

"Forgive me, Father, for I have sinned. It's been Gawd knows how long since my last confession. These're my sins: Killing my father. Being a bad father. Using the Lord's name in vain. Writing bad poems—I mean, real stink bombs. Smoking. Not drinking when I should've." Larry Rios is a lapsed Catholic; otherwise, his penance would've been a doozy. Driving to Walgreens to buy allergy medication—because San Antonio translated into English means cedar fever—"Reality Check" by Binary Star plays from his iPod. The verse *lyrical turpentine* jolts in him a poem that evanesces in the drugstore's oversaturated luminescence.

200. Unrepentant

For—and to—each of his body parts, he writes a poem. Arms. Calves. Knees. Feet. Phalanges that strangled. Organs working undercover and overtime. Sternum, that calcified middle fortress. It struck Larry Rios as though discovering his checking account emptied (not too far off) that one could construe with respectable accuracy his catalog as one long goodbye. Or a prolonged farewell. To life, to death, to love, happiness, the audience who concerned themselves. And if such were the case—it may very well be—he mustn't apologize for any of it. He might. He can't. He won't. The poet as unrepentant.

201. Long Game

And as is the case with 79% of his poetical end results, the body-parts poems are garbage. Trash. Drivel. Alas, the pursuit of poetry is baseball—you play it for the long game. The losing game. The endgame, baby. Sometimes when he's feeling bubbly—extra pep in the step—Larry Rios tags his foulest efforts, for they too, as letdowns, false starts, denizens of the majority of his dwindling time, must be honored. Thus, The Body Parts Poems, which he presently drags into a folder labeled suchly on his desktop, sandwiched between, alphabetically, The Big-Little Poems and The Count Chocula Poems.

202. Metallic Lozenge

Cruising a one-way street, the setting sun casting the horizon in a momentary otherworldly glow, Larry Rios—a resisting body on a secluded backroad on some goliath's spinning globe—imagines, not for the first time (big whoop), himself a flea tethered to a metallic lozenge sliding down a serpent's gray tongue. He thinks, If each fleabag's a first-person novel, why not make mine eyebrow-raising? He thinks, Popeye-like, How blessed I yam to be what I yam, leading the misled life, if we can't be frens we'll be emenies. He thinks of his uncle whose defective heart doomed him before his start.

203. Spring Break

Spring break of his junior year of college, he went home. Devastating, nevertheless seasonal, how brightly the colors shone; even hay-toned stretches of dead grass, soon revived, welcomed him back. All's well in a world where home's at. At the dining table, his father's face, wooden, consequently impenetrable, prefigured a difficult softening. Why didn't you call sooner? he asked. Tried to, mijo, but you couldn't be reached. Figured you were outta town. Busy. Which was true; he'd accompanied Professor Masterson to a seminar, Masterson addressing the inexpressibility of dying alone, *God is dead* equaling God is *not* dead. That old thing.

204. Unnoticed

Along the Gulf of Mexico, heavy rains. Clement winds ushering nimbostratus clouds eastbound, north. The sensation: entrapment—a reminder: hearts beat furious for so long. Temporary heat merely alluding to forever. In Larry Rios' purview, today's the breath of God. Hot exhalation, a Tongue on which biodiversity pulses. And It tugs us back to sand. Nearby his home, Larry passes by an unmissably large rust-colored building he seems to've missed, like so many things. Why? Doesn't matter. It stood unnoticed, camouflaged, heretofore flat. Two women in black pass by Larry. He doesn't know them from Eve. Shall never learn their names.

205. Third Funeral

These were the facts (from Latin *factum*, late 15th century): It was spring break of his junior year of college; the vegetation cycle endured: microcosm of our carbon-based life and times; his car was thousands of miles overdue for maintenance; he was in custody of a printout of haiku about roses; his father was alive; and gone was his mother, one with the wind. A parable. The night of her burial he bought his father a case of beer. Waited till loosening of faculties to ask him again, how? Monitoring his opaque eyes. Excepting a minor detail, the story remained unchanged.

206. Self-Sacrifice

Long ago, Larry Rios caught on that the number of units in circulation decreases the value per unit, that once a writer's words enter the world, canon, knowledgebase, ether, they're no longer hers, his assembly of symbols post-exodus to the scattering medium, they've always been someone else's—friends, foes, unclassifieds—the writer left to her thoughts, spare-tire words, nothing more, nothing less, chances are they'll fade, chances are they're already away, there's no clearer way to put this: nothing's owed to these masochists, nothing guaranteed, debts must be paid, mouths fed, morgues filled—don't conflate self-sacrifice and nobility, pain and gain.

207. Undefinable Talent

For six months he chipped away at a story, which saw unpaid publication in his university's literary journal in the fall of his senior year. Select professors (the reading type) noticed a craftsmanship that pointed toward undefinable talent despite the piece's unconventionality. The tale: an undergrad who spent untold time memorizing six dictionaries, fueling him to write—for his deceased mother—elegies and panegyrics so elaborate, so exacting, he expected God would bless him for undivided devotion. The student landed menial employment post-graduation and, following a car accident, lost 75% hearing in one ear and the inner voice of his mother.

208. Entombed

The day crisp, cloudless. Almost plagueless. Larry Rios finds a silverfish-bitten copy of the translated poetry of a Salvadoran whose work has long been outta print. Possibly faded from collective memory. Is anonymity so unfavorable? There's harmony in no longer subjecting your butt-naked words to mass scrutiny. Comprehensive oral examination. Not too dissimilar from the afterlife of a minor god. Man dumps his passions crafting pristine offerings only to become a figment recollected by weathered stone. A moss-strewn name. Miniaturized. What's left of the Salvadoran: entombed in this copy. It is said reading him in any language is a political act.

209. Strange Locales

In the spirit of Nabokov (who's everywhere all at once), let's assert the fledgling wishful thinker perceived himself a prodigal son of comeuppance who with the dispensation of libraries chomped his master's hand that fed him long after it was gone. Unstoppably, he glanced around, detected strange locales with the hieroglyphic eyes of a dreamer dreamt by a nameless sorcerer. His life, the books warned, hardly his own. He loved his father, who'd taught him chess, but what best lesson did the flushed widower save for last? You're catching your second wind, eh, Pops? The son nailing him to the culmination.

210. Statuesque Aura

Larry Rios parks near his unit, sees, again, on the second floor of the building adjacent to his, the old woman out on her balcony. For over a year he hasn't seen her otherwise—her Jackie O. sunglasses, steel hair pulled back in a bun, peach-colored silk nightgown, occasionally talking to whomever on the phone, Larry occasionally conjecturing if the other line's permanently disconnected. She lives alone. Occasionally, from afar, he waves at her, and she returns the gesture 75% of the time; the remaining quarter is written off as macular degeneration. Her statuesque aura comforts him. She's cool; he's cool.

211. Intruders

In his dream, an obnoxious knocking disrupts his reading. He opens the door to two bespectacled men of gargantuan verticality. The strangers flash a badge, abruptly duck inside, point to the caged frog in the corner. "Yuks, presumably?" "But bumpheads, he belongs to my only daughter." "Detectives," rectify the intruders. *Ribbit*, ribbits Yuks the sword-swallowing frog. The gum(platform)shoes lift the supernatural frog, exit the lodging, ask, "You familiar with the tax codes decreed on the Rosetta Stone?" "I, Nye L. Izm, one of Pessoa's lost heteronyms, plead the Fifth." "Cute. We'll have your playmate home before sunup." Carrion birds converge nearby.

212. Outrageous Act

After an unproductive workday, although one markedly relaxing, Larry Rios withdraws from a drawer a journal, jots down (never up) what's essentially his first and final entry: *Nothing to report, old sport—except the pulverized pen outside the post office. BIC Atlantis ballpoint. How do I know? Cuz we are awareness + consumerism. Also, it's the same pen (but a superior version) with which I transfigure this lined page. O! the horrors. The savaged pens; new recruits. Disciples gone amok. Every fact begetting one answer, a hundred questions. Is it sage to postpone such destinies? I'm one outrageous act away from—*

213. Mime's Honor

On their penultimate date they went for coffee and croissants. Burned calories traipsing to a necropolis of protrud-
ing tombstones like a jaw with surplus teeth. Should these
dead arise, they'll meet the eastern sun. Tina Sandiego sat
upon one headstone belonging to one *Larry Rios*, said,
C'mere, tigre. Tongues clashing for dominance, she steered
his hand to her neck. He squeezed gently, initially. Eyes
widened, mischievous. Suggestible, influençeable, irrésist-
ible, monsieur. He stared gravely at her. You'll never tell
a soul. Is that loud'n clear, Sandiego? She heard. Flashed
him a peace sign. Mime's honneur, mon amour, mime's
honneur. Oath honored. Amen.

214. Gall

You know what I can't stomach about Latin literature, or Latin-American literature, or American literature for that matter? Lucia said. What, mi amor? he wanted to know, putting down his Mario Vargas Llosa novel. Men who write women as pieces of meat to be sucked and chucked like tuna cans. For what, plot advancement? Where do y'all get the gall, the balls, to write a single word without— she paused. Y'all? he interjected. Nuh-uh, she continued, don't say it goes both ways. Then she added: Comet drew her today. Your Gorgon-haired whore. Demonic bitch. He thought: *Gall* and *balls* aren't interchangeable.

215. Distracted Ears

He peeks through his blinds—flashing lights, something black-bagged and stretchered to the ambulance rear. Larry Rios knows it's the old woman from across his building in there. It occurs to him that she must've fallen, banged her head on a table. All alone. Of course, it happened that way. Larry's overcome with melancholy old as time. His phone, half buried between sofa cushions, plays a video from ESPN. A loudmouth announcer announces, "Russian touchdown," but Larry gathers he actually announced, "Rushing touchdown." His distracted ears bending audible truth. Other realities they've effortlessly distorted, surely, those fleshy entryways jammed with wax.

216. Crepuscular Sensitivity

Proceeding his elderly neighbor's removal—(harsh word, but accurate)—he's reminded of an assignment from yesteryears, interviewing a woman who purportedly was the secret girlfriend of Jimmy Hoffa. Story like that demands superfluous—therefore nonexistent—time and resources to permit wild claims to stew until all impurities are burned, resulting in an air-tight dish safe for public consumption. Likely story. 'Twas a waste; the article was scrapped; he and his then freshly divorced editor upheld icy relations. Tonight's moon stirs in Larry Rios a crepuscular sensitivity to lost love. Love lost, which, he believes, is the falcon and egg of faith.

217. No Worries

For the fourth time today somebody tells Larry Rios, "No worries." Therefore, he's on the cusp of amping up his worrying. (Not the best or the worst idea.) He scratches out entirely—antagonistically—the first and only journal entry he'd recently penned, replacing his former words with these: *Contrarians are exhausting. Idiots are exhausting. The highly educated are exhausting. Highly educated idiots're exhausting. The examined life is exhausting. Art, iconoclasm, sensibility—exhausting. Parenting is exhausting. Parricide's exhausting. Tragedy's exhausting. Poetry's exhausting. Charity's exhausting. Coherence is exhausting. Sustenance is exhausting. Social constructs are exhausting. Social contracts—exhausting. Prudence, forgiveness, restoration—pure insanity.*

218. Pleasure

If he's 100% sincere (which is impossible), Larry Rios would say he writes poetry because he finds catharsis in the physicality of setting pen to paper, manipulating space, darkening whiteness. He abhors much of his output, nonetheless. An aspiring poetess once asked him, So you tolerate the messes that aren't yours? Larry responded, Something like that, but the complete opposite. As Larry conflates (for pleasure) the rise and apex of the novel with that of capitalism, he contemplates names for an imaginary podcast. *Softcovers with Larry Rios. Magic Mountain Biking with Larry Rios. The Heart's a Lonely Jawbreaker with Larry Rios.*

219. December Air

The December air so sharp that Larry Rios expects the skin squeezing his knuckles to assume the demeanor of mudcracks. He opens emails from two webzines informing him, in automated fashion, that his poems have unfortunately been rejected, to please submit again soon. For the first time in years, he tries his hand at a short story—about a guy who for leisure catches typos in classic and contemporary literature then contacts the respective bigwig publishers. He wrecks his marriage and friendships, leaving himself only with his job and obsessions. Larry trash-bins the story. Too autobiographical, he thinks. No, too memoiristic.

220. Interjection

If I may briefly interject (for the headspace of our spasmodically affable antihero isn't always wholly, um, cuddling), the primary reason why Larry Rios scrapped his recent short story was self-imposed limitation—censorious constraint not allowing himself to use, in his story, the words *love* and *dream*—which, in the end, he failed to accomplish, and in the end, was unaccomplishable. Incongruous. Amateurish. Like climbing K2 completely naked. (Does *naked* need the adverb *completely* preceding it? Au contraire, as they say in Pakistan.) Prejudiced, tarnished, vandalized, desecrated—nobody asked him to shoulder such escalating damages. Further confirmation that he's alive. Amen.

221. Cleansing

Massaging Head & Shoulders into his scalp, basking in the underestimated privilege of regular cleansing, Larry Rios thinks about Clark Gable, remembers hearing of the fabled film star's showering four times daily, never bathing out of fear of sitting in his own dirty water. Gable's erstwhile germaphobia and current corporeal decomposition form a blockage in Larry's mind, as if to insinuate that one disposition doesn't uphold another—past doesn't precipitate present. However, one indeed requires the passage of the other to be that which it is. To be hygienic is to someday be enclosed in decay—to be smaller than death.

222. Gaps

Larry Rios, being of semi-sound mind—analog taste—doesn't subscribe to Spotify—until today. Draped in the blues, in the mood for modern distraction. Sliding into his algorithm: Justin Timberlake's "Señorita." *Gentlemen, goodnight. Ladies, good morning.* Five slick words sunsetting a song; one verse seamlessly cultivating an alter ego, a money machine—Larry's foot tapping, steady tempo. To our quasi-murderman, the science of circuit boards and computer programming is a hefty meal to digest. Other gaps in Larry's experiential self-education: distinguishing the variances between the five major cloud roots; understanding the ethics behind manufacturing pharmaceuticals; and shamefully, how do airplanes fly?

223. Invite

An attractive colleague invites him to watch *Pan's Laby-rinth* at her place. Larry Rios replies he'd already been plowed by the inscrutable artwork of Leonora Carrington. Blank stare. "Work's got me in a chokehold," he snaps silence with a kernel of truth. His colleague doesn't investigate what's Leonora Carrington got to do with it; Larry leaves unexplained the last-standing Surrealist's overarching influence—her striking resemblance to his mother. Larry's colleague will never extend another opportunity to connect with our resident hot mess. Larry maintains his front-facing sangfroid. Mexican hallucinations, he thinks later. One-way streets to the ramparts of Hell. No gracias.

224. Filch, Inject

It was such a Lucia habit to filch the fiction from his bespoke books, inject it into their married dream. Balancing poetry's checkbook? she inquired the week he tackled Nicanor Parra's *Poems and Antipoems*. Or: Has our enlightened moron repeated history so soon? re: his three weeks with Dostoevsky's *The Idiot*. Or: Three's a crowd and two too many re: his three summer evenings with Gertrude Stein's *Three Lives*. Or (thrice daily for as many days, pinching her nose): Toilet bowl cleaner's under the sink—Cortázar's *Blow-Up and Other Stories*. What he wouldn't give for an encore. Guiltless repartee. Kisses goodnight.

225. Final Chat

He wakes to him lying on his side, facing him, Reclining Buddha, lips curled faintly. Before he can compute, the other speaks first. "Don't startle. Just here to bid adieu." The specter of James Baldwin—the nerve of him to smoke in bed. "Jimmy, what the fudge, man?" What he meant was: It is I who seeks you. "Remember, breathe that truth, even if you're drowning. And you don't choose your idols. Mostly, you never get to know them if you're lucky. Godspeed, baby." Before vanishing, he reminds Larry Rios to feed his fish—and himself, too, for good goddamned measure.

226. Breach

From the drive-thru window Tam hands him his Italian roast, asks, "Can you believe what happened?" "Bonkers," she can't resist continuing, "the police let 'em do it!" Larry glances at his rear-view mirror—nobody tailgating. He pontificates, mock-Machiavellian: "Not only did they expect the breach, they sanctioned it. No purer way to castrate entitled crazies than to let 'em march into their own noose. You don't martyr whitey with bullets; you photograph 'im then feed 'er to the Matrix." Tam, put off, wishes Larry a *fun*tastic day. Later, he'll present her an apology giftcard, "To the pursuit of Happiness, that flirt."

227. Unreal

Larry Rios reads a short story about a police rat—literally, a rat that's a policeman. He surmises that the only real thing is story—words left behind. Signposts. Rat droppings. Mousetraps. "Nothing else exists," Larry mutters. "Nothing else matters. Then what?" He's on the verge of quitting smoking again, fondly recalling the time he and Tina Sandiego smoked a book of poetry. Literally, after co-turning a page, they tore it from the collection, burned it, mixed its ashes with hash. Unreal, he thinks. But literally all true. Sacrebleu. He's jonesing for a cigarette. For more than he can bargain for.

228. Metabolize

And the fact is he can't remember the doggone title of the book they'd smoked, removed from circulation, in spite of his meticulous recall, in spite of the predictable dilemma of memory, in spite of the phantasmagoria he contracted in Mexico (despite his will), despite Lucia once loving him, his daughter once knowing him (tangibly), his being worthy, once, of that capricious virtue called love, that which, twisted, metabolizes into a penchant for flame-watching (not pyromania, exactly, but close). Larry Rios is a murderer. Watched his father go up in flames. His work eradicated (atomized) in the pyre of his body.

And if the only real thing is story, then Larry Rios' story is summed in the following sentence: *A boy becomes a man becomes someone else, while his library grows while his cognizance shrivels.* If story's the only real thing, becoming a poet extraordinaire is other than extraordinary; it's the only reasonable outcome. If Entropy's the guiding principle of life—stars and flesh its ride or dies—its sworn enemy is the Fountain of Youth—Fire the ultimate double-agent, the enviable counterspy, the Mole for All Times. If story's the only real thing, what'd you call books everlastingly returned to dust?

230. Rehash

This story summarized in the following sentence: *Larry Rios (before the change) was privileged with two loving parents, therefore fated to be lost without them someday.* In OutKast's dancefloor-filling song, "Hey Ya!", André 3000 wisely states (as stated in Chapter 133): *Thank God for Mom and Dad / For sticking two together / 'Cause we don't know how.* Before the burning of his father, he dreamt of a funeral parlor wherein his father knelt before his mother's casket. Gone too soon, his father said. No coming back. Inside the coffin wasn't his mother, though—it was The Snake-Haired Lady's severed head.

231. Unfolded

In the coffin The Snake-Haired Lady opened her serpent's mouth, sunk her serrated fangs into his groin, his testicles gone forever, no going back—his parents' place ascending, Dad's toolbox melting to liquid. The nightmare prompted him to ask his father to lunch to attain closure, to learn finally the cause of his mother's death, and if Dad still wrote secretive poems to the girl he'd killed in Vietnam. He believed his right to get to the crux. To be owed proper explanation. At lunch his father surprised him, unfolded a sheet of paper, allowed him to read his latest work.

232. Ironic Slap

Larry Rios writes a poem about a rags-to-riches woman who graduates from accumulating found objects to expansive works of art (the likes of which she confidentially desires to saw in half). He writes another poem about a riches-to-rags man whose extensive art collection is gambled, squandered. The two meet at an exhibit, where the woman, against instincts, begins rehabilitating the man, eventually becoming a diamond. One poem about Jesus; the other, lambs. Kentucky-based magazine, *Amphibious Libido*, on the verge of folding, publishes them. They reject, ironically, Larry's other poem featuring Yuks the sword-swallowing frog. Life's one ironic slap on the ass.

233. Novel Procedure

The word *evidence* creeps to the forefront of his attention. Circumstantial evidence, prefigurations of arcane puzzles. Ongoing investigations. One massive riddle. Feedback loop with so much utopian input, so many nihilist restrictions, you can't begin to pinpoint where the head begins, the tale ends. Larry Rios is shook, most of what he's heard being apocryphal, filtered, the worst having already occurred, the most horrific—yet to arrive. He's forced his way out of today's work, an ejection he can live with. He'll survive, for now. Pay attention. We're not done here. There's no novel way to proceed. The procedure is live.

234. Novel Procedure

Larry Rios checks the safe under his bed. Cracking open the signed copy of *Giovanni's Room*, he finds a snubbed cigarette having pretty much snuffed out the author's priceless inscription to William Styron—Larry with zero recollection of discarding recklessly, barbarically, a firestick there—the source code of a sagely wraith—which pretty much explains his adieu. In some antechamber in his noggin, Larry, whose margin of error is thinning vis-à-vis all things organic, decides it's time for a change, although what?, is the question. How to proceed. He contemplates the meaning of the phrase *novel procedure*. The needle scantly moves.

235. Thirty Seconds

As he carefully, composedly, read his father's poem—comprised of alexandrines devoted shockingly, then unsurprisingly, to the girl he'd shot in Vietnam—he couldn't resist marveling at the bucolic imagery, precision of syllables marching a dignified, unflappable pace. They're alexandrines, his father said, to which his chip off the old block replied: Commendable, before letting go and commenting: You're a natural. Then the strangest line left his father's lips: Thirty seconds is all it takes to know everything you need to know about a person, but spend a dreamlife with them, you'll still know them as little as you know yourself.

236. The Management

"What cloudy climes for poetry," Larry Rios says to a leafless tree whose branches are like black veins raring to connect with a gray expanse they can't quite, will never, reach. He slips on his brown Chucks, cardigan that makes him feel Hemingwayesque. Halfway through morning joe, responding curtly to work emails, biting his maudlin tongue, that earlier spellbinding predilection has formally lost its luster. Within our Larry-sized matryoshka doll nests a cantankerous, unquestionably unpublishable collection titled *Gallows Humor*, wherein seven lengthy poems (one for each organ without which the body cannot survive) each culminate in a glacial punchline: *The Management*.

237. Generating Ideas

And if story's the only real thing, there's no time, then, for time, death to champions, death to losers, death to radicals, parasites, paramours, pacifists, anachronists, altruists, alpinists, chefs, commas cannibals proletariats hackers deuteragonists exiles statisticians senators philanthropists philanderers forefathers beauticians micromanagers generals coconspirators chemists conformists botanists wanderers weasels werewolves marauders freelancers no-collars necrophiliacs impersonators scattered stars white noise—death to the Void, death to forgotten children, death to medusas, death to heroes empresarios morticians poetry, obituary of demolished mirrors. Obituary of demolished mirrors—that has a polished ring to it, Larry Rios muses. I must write. While time yet clings.

238. Self-Reckoning

"My g-g-God," Larry Rios stammers, "could it be this whole time I've classified myself Chicano Poet Extraordinaire my aim was to get … distinguished? No way, Jose. But what's the point elsewise? What's the impetus beyond the unbearable wreckage of me, sliver by sliver, cut by cut the self-inflicted lingchi the speed of snails, the acquired tartly aftertaste like escargot? What about the intolerable chasm between father and son, daughter and father? What about the Japanese saying: The nail that sticks up will be hammered down? Welcome to Texas, compadre. Welcome to the valley of rusty nails bulging out like …!"

239. It

The rain noncommittal, drizzle. Larry Rios without a clue as to how he's done it. How anyone has. It—actions building upon actions. Weighting. Submerging. Revising. He folds his shirts, wipes his ceiling fan, plans his next play—not without minimal exertion. It's obvious, isn't it, the checkpoint between doing and thinking? Violations of second-guessing. Misdirections of unaccredited schools of Why. Larry's certain there're only four categories of story in this world: 1) a lot happens with everything at stake; 2) a lot happens with nothing at stake; 3) nothing happens with everything at stake; 4) nothing happens, nothing at stake.

240. Hand

So it was, at lunch with his father, after rereading his poem, he asked the waitress for a pen, marked an alexandrine here, an alexandrine there, crossed a few words out, added some in without compromising the syllable count. He slid the paper back to his father, who studied the revisions, nodded, said, You're the natural, mijo. A few days later, the guilt of complicity, of collaboration, corroboration, flooded everything in him with sleep-robbing ingredients. As though he'd let himself, beguilingly, morph into the pen in his father's hand—his father's hand itself, with at least one body to its name.

241. Love Letters

In Enrique Vila-Matas' meta-novel, *Bartleby & Co.*, the Spaniard writes: *Literature was precisely—the same was true for Kafka—the only means I had to try to become independent of my father.* In Alejandro Zambra's *Ways of Going Home*, the Chilean writes: *The novel belongs to our parents, I thought then, I think now.* Both novels' narrators are versions of their meta-creators who share a hulking mother tongue dispatching love letters to Mom and Pops. Dear reader, isn't this true of all literature? That it's all a dream of a love letter in which our parents are resurrected with unidentifiable fingerprints?

242. Shakespeare and Cervantes

1) Least number of words a writer can allot a character to illuminate everything about her? 2) Tree falls in the woods, a Hispanic hears it, therefore folklore. Tree falls in the woods, a gringo hears it, therefore undisputable truth. Tree falls in the woods, a frog hears it, therefore silent trauma. 3) One hundred? 4) Leaning against his bookshelf, dreaming of being squashed by books. 5) Twenty-three? 6) Everything askew, everything flatlined under the heel of time. 7) Seven? 8) Everything strewn, everything spewed under the heel of time. 9) Hopeless Romantic Redundancy Department. 10) Ten. 11) April 23, 1616.

243. Straw

Overnight, it seemed, his father shed twenty pounds. Weakness. Blood. Deterioration inside out. Retribution of warfare. Orange ghosts. At once, it seemed, he'd soon join his mother, whatever that meant, however it'd play out. Unfair, how fury was sucked from this emerging man, this son. Extracted as though through a straw, as though from an unseeable monster. You don't demand answers from those who've *been* the horrors. He called his father, who greeted him: Hello, my Poet Extraordinaire. Pops, I'm a prose writer, don't you get it? And the father said: Write for those who can't—write for those who won't.

244. Worked Up

Jeez Louise, what's got Larry Rios so worked up? Two things: 1) Anticipating which word'll be the last written by the last writer; 2) Opening a work email with a single noun for a subject line, no salutation, one sentence in the body—a question: *Where are we on this?* "Where are we on this," Larry status-checks the drywalls of his living room. "Where are we on this," venomous emphasis on *we, this*. The age of devaluation. The age of the thankless factotum. Age of kindergarten prattle. Age of faux nonconfrontational hardball. All for what, a pathetic merit raise, fingers crossed?

245. Five Prospects

While Larry Rios is powerless to resolve the problem of horrendous email etiquette—nor should it be his concern—he lands on five prospects that could hold the distinction of being the last words ever written by the last writer. They are: farewell, goodbye, Godspeed, adios, 再见. Obviously, this dubious selection implies cultural bias—would the last writer really sign off in English, Spanish or Chinese? Statistically speaking, correctamundo. Now if I may—I insist—I prefer the delightful *Godspeed*. The cessation of writing encapsulated on a sporting note. Movement insinuated, divine, long after the written word's dried up.

246. Dumbest Thing

The dumbest thing happens this morning. Larry Rios, brushing his chompers, regarding his reflection, reflects, What might a dust mote like moi do in a folktale? He extends his arm toward his facsimile's mouth, emits toothily, "Burt's bees!" Brushes its teeth, soiling his mirror schoolboy-like, oafishly. (Even *Home Alone* Macauley Culkin behaves better than this.) But here's the dumber thing: Larry thinks solely of story, his harebrained behavior serving exclusively the function of time-removed documentation. Which he's accomplishing. A poem piloting its own poesy to the frontier of: Who's scrubbing whose face? The citizenry, here? They lay out their cards cavalierly.

247. Vultures

The paradox here being that characters in folktales making choices page after page are all the while downright choiceless all the livelong day, helpless negating the prison sentences (pun) of their makers. Sentences inverted. Before this morning, Larry Rios hadn't quite framed it this way. "Dang," he says, "this Chicano Poet Extraordinaire bidness is suspect shiz." I've seen it writ that poets are the ingrate vultures of civilization, nibbling carrion remnants of cold texts. This much is true: Presently, you're not quite yourself again. Less of you left to recover for future reconnaissance missions. So seize what's yours and savor it.

248. Ten Words

Deploying the last of his Barbasol, Larry Rios reflects on the fortitude of folks in antiquity. He wantonly renders his neck raw and pink as a plucked chicken's. (What's razor burn, discomfort, this far along?) Don't cry. Machismo (a brittle costume) the likes of which Zapata stashed 'neath his 'stache. Then a sentence thrashes Larry like a shearing bolt from Zeus: *He does some of the job some of the time.* Ten words: the least number of words needed to illuminate everything about a character, mas o menos, in this free country—freeways revealing our patterns, only to find freedom wanting.

249. Reemergence

The Sunday sky the color of sherbert—a midcentury dessert shade from the post-Sabbath, star-studded macrocosm, onerous and confounding—as Larry Rios attempts yet again to pin down the meaning of love's trajectory. Love's trajectory, he contemplates, is like looking at a photograph of your ex from y'all's wedding night. Like looking at a crumpled cutout of your Hollywood crush in their prime. Love's trajectory, pray tell, is masturbating to a memory, an extended omission, an eyes-closed reddish apparition of your soulmate. Then, from the unfamiliar number (read: Chapter 195), another text arrives. *Brother. Call soon?* Nelson. He did call it.

250. Weird Convo

"If it ain't my favorite fuzz." "Brother. Sorry to reemerge like a bashful turtle, but got something to tell you. Urgent request, really." "All earlobes, Donatello." "If you use me sometime in a story or novel—" "I'm a poet exclusively these days," Larry amends, "but I'll consider it." "In a vignette, a prose poem—all I ask is you tell the truth. Nothing but. Strip search it. Am I being crystal?" "Nope. Use more fudgin' words, Nelly." "Look, don't minimize me as a cypher for bogus morality. Use me good. But make it spectacular." "Ten-four. I'll use you spectacularly, then."

"Thanks. You're a regular Victor Hugo." "Naw—better. How's the jay-oh-bee? The wifey?" "Short story shorter, I quit the force. And she's due next month, can you believe?" "Whoop there it is! Hallelujah, Daddy-o." "But we're not married anymore. She's pleased as punch now, trust me." "Lord. That's swell. You lousy scoundrel." "Up yours, Lare-Bear. Say, we'll find our way one way or noway. The story flies above us, eh?" "No kiddin'. The Story's the clouds and then some." "Amen. Remember: make me spectacular." "Ten-four. Consider your *roman clef*'d. Remember: life's a romp. Death's a rump. Laugh now—crap out later."

252. Sidenote

(The following's much ado about nothing. Skip to the next section at your discretion, at your own risk.) Larry Rios drops by a used bookshop (used-books shop?). He doesn't like admitting this but he's there to procure lawfully a manhandled copy of Cormac McCarthy's *All the Pretty Horses*. It's not the paperback's laughable condition—folded in two—that attracts him. It's the passage highlighted on Page 43: *You think they got vienna sausages in Mexico?* No markups elsewhere. Larry hardly buys marked-up books. Hardly makes exceptions. As to the highlighted question on Page 43, he can answer it with 100% conviction.

253. Liquefying

"I'm somebody with nobody sensibilities. Somebody liquefying into nobody." The bright 'n' early mutterings of Larry Rios, Poet Extraordinaire. Today somebody; tomorrow nobody. If the kids had it their way, they'd be invincible, pick a decade, it's the wonder years somewhere. Once upon a time, a young buck believed he was indestructible. Hopped straight onto time's bent arrow the night he noticed his first patch of melanin-starved hair, a finish-line glimpse, inspiring a barrage of text passed as an existential-crisis story. Which his father read, observing that it hit too close to home. If I want real life, I walk outside.

254. Sidenote Addendum

Right after Larry Rios whips out his credit card to buy the maltreated copy of *All the Pretty Horses*, the cashier—heavyset fella with a majestic white beard—says, "Paying with Mr.Plastic?" Larry eyes him for a second, determines his airy colloquialism is of the variety that sprouts only in this neck of the woods. "Yessir," Larry says, "but d'ya think he'll cover the damages that really matter?" The cashier—whose ruddy countenance signifies something charitable but pugnacious—responds, "What's your credit limit?" "Too small. Too big. Just right." Larry departs the indie bookshop jauntily, having fathered this infinitesimal ripple.

255. Scars

Blessed is the body marred with scars, enduring Earth's ferocity. His right knee was the bad one, damaged years ago from league basketball—ACL tear—reinjured one morning hopping outta bed, legs stretched and locked, Comet—barely three feet tall—wandering into their still-shaded bedroom, bumping into him at an angle. He collapsed onto his bed clutching his knee, knocking Comet over, poor girl. He shifted his torso to pick his daughter up off the floor. She was bawling. It's okay, baby, he comforted. It's alright. In that instant she developed the irreversible sense she was capable of hurting her dad.

256. Passion Project

(Listen, ain't it time we consider we're God's passion project?) He was reaching for his thirties when he read Rilke's *Letters to a Young Poet*. Remembers thinking on an escalator (escaping entanglement yet again): Solitude—*deep aloneness*—evolution—you can play armchair Darwin all the livelong day. Remembers agreeing with Rilke that criticism's inconsequential to art. (Rilke, still reaching for his thirties—we forget, how young were our dead). To Larry Rios, youth isn't wasted on the young; it's discarded by the weary. *The future stands still ... but we move in infinite space.* Speedily enough to collide into the past.

257. Future

If the future isn't something we move toward but that which moves toward us, assumes control like a proxy, we've already changed, the future is grief, the untraceable barrier into which we drift as boots on ice, pull of the deep-marine, the Void, the selfsame presence infecting the flower shop owner off Woodlawn who opens up to Larry Rios that he'll be buried in the refrigerator he'd purchased from a World War I veteran. Changing subjets: "Try this line on a special woman: 'It's a blessing being part of your story.' If that don't work, I'm a character in a book."

258. Web Surfing

Larry Rios dreams of petting a horse on an open prairie, but the horse neighs and kicks while Larry can't seem to stay out of its way. The next day, he aimlessly surfs the annals of Google (or rather the internet's monetized anal cavity) and chances upon an image of a sandwich board with the words: *Our books are feeling mighty lonely. Come inside and tickle them.* "N'ombre!" Larry bellows. Try as he might, he cannot disengage; forty-five minutes are surrendered in a blink. The horse, he recalls, was gray, and a multiplying number of facts are at his disposal. Great.

259. Complimentary

For a little while, not too long—for these things cannot last long—he shared his stories with his ailing father under the guise of partnership. Something like it, far from it. If he couldn't ask him direct questions, he'd depose them, lock them up in the diseased cell of so-called fiction. His story titles were ambiguous, evasive, underdeveloped: "Rigama-role," "Peashooter," "Impetuousness." By the third story the body count surpassed ten, the matriarchal figures unfailingly ending up lifeless. Contrary to expectations, his father's compliments were upbeat, buoyant. These stories are by the hand of an original Poet. An approval. A cautioning.

260. Reinforcement

Come see something, his father said. From his closet he retrieved a shoebox, from the shoebox removed a softball of browned newsprint, from the newsprint the Colt Detective Special, which seemed to announce itself in the shrillest of whispers, that small assemblage of black snubnosed metal whose singular commitment was reinforcing the law of Chekhov's gun, his father's war trophy, his hand reassuming quite naturally the form of this resuscitated armament whose lineage, he informed his son, traced back to a buddy from 'Nam, a tunnel rat from Louisiana who'd scarcely experienced his first kiss before firing the revolver only once.

261. Voluptuous Ruptures

Larry Rios dreams he befriends Nobel Prize in Literature awardee Louise Glück, who's energetic, dreamy, starved for companionship, poetry; she's alive, and she reads Larry's uncategorizable manuscripts at implausible speed, faster than full-time slackworms up against 11:59 p.m. deadlines. She digs his work, the shape of his poems amid whitewalls of boneyard muteness she calls "voluptuous ruptures," to which Larry fibs that that was the name of his garage punk band—Voluptuous Ruptures. Louise proceeds to ask about his ex, his daughter, but he frets because he notices she's already sighted, her Cambridge eyes so worn and animated, his unplucked unibrow.

262. Inner Weather

At the cemetery he kneels before the grave, trappings of his inner weather (*Inner Weather*: a graceful poetry collection by a driven and calamitous Denis Johnson) shoving him someplace disorienting, headrush visions of a crucifix submerged in seaweed. Head planted in the receding grass, he weeps soundlessly, this man with the name not christened by the parentage disintegrating beneath him, facing fixed terms. On this rotisserie sphere, his sweet girls won't be buried next to him. Larry Rios feels like all his limbs are borrowed—stolen—callously used, abused. A branch snapped off the tree. Spanish moss. Touch it and see.

263. Socked

The lights are on but the poetry's off. The lights're on but the poetry's odd. The light's off but Poetry's a disco ball in an empty dance hall in Texas where the scarlet sun secretes her secrets nightly. Poetry: a gangster's foot pressing the gas or pumping the brakes of his Crown Vic. On YouTube, Larry Rios listens to Jim Croce's "You Don't Mess Around With Jim," remembering when Comet once said she wanted to see Jim Croce sing live. He died long ago in a plane crash, her father said. Wishing someone else had socked the excitement right outta her.

264. Big If

What he adored and therefore dreaded about Lucia was her facility to pose hard-hitting questions so unblinkingly, so without hiccup, it made you speculate if she wasn't a psychopath in some other string-cheese galaxy. After a dinner of ravioli and baked broccoli—a rather complimentary coupling—she said, If, and I know this is a big if, amor, if Comet were to die, but we had time to prepare for it, where would you like to take her? He choked on spit, but not before contemplating the evening skyline, which appeared a jagged row of bottom teeth meets toothless sapphire abyss.

265. Wee Challenger

Too long his chess set amasses dust, so in the two minutes his cup of water microwaves for instant coffee, Larry Rios wets a paper towel, wipes down the board, the aftermath of soil eliciting his satisfactory response, "Yes, here I've been awhile." He hears his father's counsel—*always cherish your queen*—remembers passing that on to Comet while processing, still, how he'd misguided her. What if all my pieces are gone? she asked. I win, he answered. And what if I still got my queen? She protects her king. Presently, it appears as though Larry's pretending he's playing his betta.

266. Best Somethings

If you're fortuitous enough to live a full life, live fully, you'll deliver, at some point, yes you will, the best something—best somethings—the best joke, comeback, lie, prayer, poem, kiss, thrust, offspring—after which, by definition, subsequent performances won't eclipse—astatine snapshots of time. Take, for instance, Kiefer Sutherland's best line on film—1987's *The Lost Boys*—directed toward actor Jason Patric upon his refusal, as Michael Emerson, to consume steamed rice before its transmutation to maggots (or vice versa): *Tell me, Michael, how could a billion Chinese people be wrong?* '80s vampires, Larry Rios thinks. "Bloodthisrty Ronald Reagans."

267. Phone Call

A phone call, middle of night (as if night, in its fathomless continuity, is a midriff)—or day's end, the colossal night removing its rueful disguise. A hesitant hello. Mijo, his father greeted assuredly, incomprehensibly, maybe. I miss your mom. I miss her terribly. But it was God's will, His infinite wisdom. It's okay, be angry with me. Remember when we sent you to Mexico to stay with Grandpa? Lemme speak. It was because I had to finish something. But I couldn't. I failed. Then later when you couldn't be reached. But we're talking now. Because we can. Isn't that something?

268. Good Son

And like a good son—the good son—he listened, peered down intermittently at his scribble, a story's opening, narrative roaming anywhere—*Once in my life have I devoted to the shooting range, a falsehood, and I know you're thinking heinous paper men, spent shell casings, the aroma of thunderous death*—and he listened, not interjecting, muzzled, the good son, role of a lifetime, mask among many, a giant ear, appalling appendage, hand with a withering pen, recorder of misdeeds, failed starts, rough landings, the father speaking, confiding, but let's not call it a confession, the air of paterfamilias. Obedient heir.

269. 9:27 a.m.

It's 9:27 a.m. and Larry Rios decides with a scorned lover's swiftness that 9:27 a.m. is the most perilous of timestamps—because ten minutes after 9:27 a.m. it's 9:37 a.m., three minutes from 9:40 a.m. and 9:40 a.m. is twenty minutes from 10 a.m., and by 10 a.m. it's an hour until 11 a.m.—so-called late morning, subsisting for 3,600 seconds—then bam! Morning's donezo. See ya mañana, optimistically. The birds'll keep chirping but the chirping'll hit differently. Larry consults his watch: 9:30 a.m. Not in the plan. And for all his ambition, he cannot recover the world with his words.

270. Checkmate

Her skill level apropos of life experience, she didn't position her knight to shield her king. He slid his bishop—checkmate. Body turned, she was humiliated. Comet, he said sternly. Face me. When you scraped your elbow yesterday, you were brave. No tears. So there won't be none right now. In your future—here, he almost choked up—you'll face defeats harder than this. But you'll be better than me, so you won't ever lose. Winners are the coolest losers. He taught her how to throw a left hook in case of extreme threat. This, she came to define as grace.

271. Unvanilla

He was aware of Lucia's ocular insecurity. At the start, he didn't bring attention to those eyes. Perceptiveness, politeness—they appear handsome on a man. But like any well-adjusted hubby, he wasn't wired to not behave unstiffly for long, knowing well that stiffness would someday indissolubly claim his body. Life's shorter than a period. He indulged himself at her heterochromia's expense. Poked fun. But don't believe for a nanosecond she didn't reciprocate, clap back, starting with his hairy hobbit patas. Nobody could accuse the couple of being vanilla. She loved him. Because why else come back? Love's shorter than a period.

272. Hearty Comparison

Sometimes Larry Rios feels as if his heart's balling itself into a revolutionary fist, which sounds stylish and allegorical, but trust me, apprehensive reader, the consequential sharp (but mercifully short-lived) stabbing pains are no joke. Larry compares his heart to the legendary comedy duo of Laurel & Hardy, as though it were two vastly opposing entities—stringier left ventricle trotting into right, porkier right ventricle galloping into left. A bloody slapstick collision inside his chest. "Hmm," Larry ponders aloud. "There's a poem here, undoubtedly, cliché and, excruciating as it were, Greek. Greek salad—when's the last time you've eaten your veggies?"

273. Online Dating

Larry Rios tries the online dating thing. It's asking a lot of strangers when your profile pic is Gene Wilder as Willy Wonka. (Godspeed, Mr. Wilder.) But with Larry's peculiarly literary and finely crafted introductory paragraphs, he secures a casual coffee hangout with a cautious librarian just incautious enough to also give this online dating thing a whirl. Call it statistics. When asked his favorite genre of films, Larry replies, "Neo-noir." And the weirdest state he's visited? "Kentucky." "Lexington?" Clarice specifies. "Louisville," Larry clarifies. "Larry Rios," she says, sipping chamomile tea. "Four syllables. Nice and even." And totally fabricated, Larry thinks.

274. Deactivate

When asked why Kentuckians are exceptionally weird, Larry Rios replies they're like Texans if Texans were held upside down—unnaturally red-faced, hospitable but territorial, something intangibly awry behind the eyes. (It's always behind the eyes.) Clarice decides Larry's an iceberg (lots underneath those muddy green eyes). She too is divorced, wistful. Larry thinks: O! our plight. "Kids?" he asks. "No," she says bittersweetly. Later, he realizes he never asked for her last name; intuitively, he knows the indignity is felt. And so, he deactivates his account. Spineless mien smothered in a pillow, he tries recalling the fragrance of his daughter's hair.

275. Nickelback

Larry Rios isn't moping tonight emptyhanded. He throws on Levi's, drives to the gas station. His jeans, plausibly, feel like leg prisons—a phrase he plucked from some bookseller's banter. He leaves the store with cigarettes—swears he's quitting next month—and a Snickers bar. Come Again, the phantom-trumpet-playing slash multi-instrumentalist homeless Homo sapien, leans against Larry's car. Larry's sulking instantly dispels. He hands Come Again two nickels—clearing out his pockets. "That nickel's wack as hell," Come Again informs Larry. "But it's two nickels," Larry modulates. "Sheeit, I'll give you two nickels back to … sheeit, Nickelback's wack as hell."

276. Vile

There're hardly words. He'll be less certain from here on out that the betta was alive when he left. Bruce Lee was his first and only fish—the absolute best. (It's true—cognitive dissonance is today's katzenjammer.) He flushes Bruce Lee. Constructs in his head a poem: "The night the dragon died, again." Another one unqualified to drawing breath. In bed, he spots her there in the shadows, fixed, wrathful, an isosceles density. *I've come to eat your cock*, The Snake-Haired Lady hisses. *I'll never die.* "I know kung fu, bitch." He wonders, halfway tranquilly, who she'd once been. Tasteful—innocent?

277. Concession

You think those stories're all your own, boy? Think those words belong to you? His father's deployment of *boy*, not mijo, a rancorous tell—pointed like his Adam's apple he stroked when provoked, which didn't belong to him, surely. And what did? (But what really did?) Not the tales. Not the concealed stanzas. Not his body or blood. Not the gun. The fire. Demons of deranged Mexico. She's got me too, boy, his father conceded. All my nights. You have no idea how deep this goes. What could he say to that? Nothing. Stolen air. Carbon dioxide. Nothing warm whatsoever. Nothing.

278. Vandalism

(Are discovered poems intended to be forgotten? History made only to be effaced? Apologies—philosophizing out loud. Don't mind me.) In the men's room in a various art museum in a various building situated invariably in the city's pulsing heart, Larry Rios, drying his hands to a state of Saharan moisturelessness, notices two words etched—cut, crudely carved—on a chrome-plated hand dryer: *HONESTY, GULP*. Welp. This can only explain so many things. A hundred connotations minimum, if he puts his noodle to it. Which he won't. What kind vandalizes restrooms in the name of poetry? It's gulp-inducing. And almost honorable.

279. Impressive Physics

Following an inordinately lengthy session Wikipediaing the finer points of Taoist philosophy pertaining to the natural environment, Larry Rios tosses his phone on the sofa. Miraculously—more likely impressive physics—it lands vertically, Apple logo upside down. Forbidden knowledge on its head. Larry's filled with urgent desire to photograph the occurrence. But with what? he wonders. Desire: the chemical scar of an aching body. *All adrenaline & erupting pores.* To whom does that line belong? (But really, do lines stay faithful to us for long?) He asks himself if he's fed his fish—reminds himself his fish is dead. Silly goose.

280. Pen Pal

An email arrives from Larry Rios, Larry Rios' infrequent pen pal from California. *Dear doppelgänger—another one. Best from the muses. L.* Larry's come to value, even yearn for these irregular check-ins, their unwavering brevity. *Let one guy in / if you wish to die. Let all the guys in / to the party, let's all die.* He composes the following valediction and sends it to his namesake: *It is too late / too early for the grave. L.* They shall never meet. Their game won't produce a victor. What a dream life. Fiction's as strange as reality—then there's poetry.

281. Running Thoughts

Who'll save the writers? *Who's gonna save my soul now?* Gnarls Barkley? James Brown? Bueller? Bueller? (Are souls in North Korea allowed to be saved? Allowed to jog the streets of Pyongyang?) Work saves. Glib sex protects. Carpet burns. Erotic entries. Cover them up. Cart 'em away. Circumnavigate. Humiliate. Titillate. Unfurl. Distention. Praise Allah. Ma, do ya miss me? Mother Mary, kiss me? Who's saving our soul now? What did poetry redeem for me? Look where we landed us. Flight's delayed. Terror in the air. Boot in da sordid derriere. Bruised soles. Larry Rios sprints. Any exercise is better than none.

282. Torn Page

He entered his father's house—his father's, not his parents' anymore. On the coffee table in the living room he saw a page torn from a book whose words he didn't recognize—Page 67 of an English translation of *Poem of the Cid*, on which was the verse, disconcerting, underlined in red: *Cid commanded that no man who'd earned anything in his service / might go without first taking leave of the Cid, and kissing his hand, / otherwise he'd be run down and, if possible, seized, all / his goods taken from him and / himself impaled on a stake.*

283. Taken

Sunday morning. Bright and cool. Larry Rios stretches his legs, his back, takes a walk. He feels reasonably well, head airier than usual. Five minutes into his walk and he thinks, How wonderful it is to walk on a bright cool morning. One foot after the other. Stepping into one thought after another. Another. Life is doing what others have done and can no longer do—someday soon I'll be one among them. Larry knows the feeling won't last long. For this is us. And so, for now, mesmerized, he's unreservedly absorbed. Taken. Sati—what the Buddhists call mindfulness. Sumptuous word.

284. Overhears

Walking back to his place, the ethereal phase of mindfulness having faded in the waning cool morning, Larry Rios passes by two boyish and rangy men on a sidewalk deep in conversation. They seem on friendly terms. Friends. Mid-colloquy, Larry overhears them incognito. [Latino guy]: "Bruh, come through. I'll hook you up with that employee discount." [Black guy]: "Word, but y'all's food be hella spicy. I prefer pedestrian bowel movements." [Latino guy]: "Truthfully, I wouldn't eat our food if I didn't work there. Gives my ass mad stomachaches." (As if stomachaches arrived in better moods.) Noticing their eavesdropper, they relocate indifferently.

285. Souvenir

His father in bed under the covers, hair unkempt, eyes sunken and bombed out. He thought how Professor Masterson, in his voracious quest for knowledge, must've encountered many faces like this. In his father's right hand, the Colt Detective Special. His dead war buddy's from Vietnam. Souvenir. Just cleaning it, mijo, don't worry, he said. No such thing as a clean war. I ever tell you what happened over there? The true nature of Uncle Sam? Coverups? No, he thought—come to think of it, you haven't told much of anything. He held the torn-out page before his father. No explanation.

286. Confessional

His father told him about December 3, 1967. Hue. 0400 hours. Gunshot. Young woman in my arms. Strands of her hair mud-pasted on my rifle. Human bicycle streamers. My lieutenant kicking a mother and son into a ditch. Putting bullets in their brains. Foes everywhere. Child spies. Traps. What were we doing out there? Sometimes I hear Bob Dylan and think, I was too detached from his vision. He never sung for dirt-eyed boys like me, Uncle Sam's accidents, his subalterns. Later, anytime he hears Bob Dylan, he remembers his father under the covers. Emaciated. Confessional. A house with no windows.

The revelation illuminated his father's writings, but still not his mother's passing. As if intercepting this, his father said: Despite what happened to your tío John, it wasn't genetics that took her. It was that thing. I saw her. She was there. He put down his pistol, useless in the face of real danger. Face brooding like Edward James Olmos'. *Blade Runner.* This stops here. God is good. Eyes closed, reopened— brutal boiling beads. Fight fire with fire—you'll burn me down. That's an order. And his son thought: You're dying, now you let me in. She should've taken you, too.

288. Reaffirmed

Get the fuck outta here, he told his dad—the first and last he'd curse him out. Not now, his father said. Later, when the signal's clear … don't think. Insane, he thought. Gross and insane. I'd not ask you to do this if I could myself, his father said. She feeds off meaninglessness. But should you do it, it'd mean everything. Closing his eyes again, his father reaffirmed: Later. Soon. Give it room to breathe. Everything I have is yours, mijo. Make it look like something else. Make it mean everything. But don't think. Don't even think about thinking, boy.

289. Perfect Woman

Been ages since he's enjoyed a woman's clasp. When did he last see his ex? His daughter? He knows—the memory's pitted but not insubstantial. But what days were they, exactly? Larry Rios isn't adept at remembering dates. (We've all got our cons.) It's the kind of loose writing zone in which he conceptualizes the—a—perfect woman. Her name appearing instantly: Señora Schadenfreude. Coarse but rousing on the southwestern tongue. Mexican-German mysterious. Abstruse. A parasol-wielding madonna who slips a matchbox in your hand. Lights one another into another life. She sports a Frida Kahlo tee. Is comfortable with the unknown.

290. Breathtaking Word

As this account draws near conclusion—for our narrative lens cannot fix permanently on our wearied pro-agonist, it just cannot—another intermission: There's a word in the English language I believe is breathtaking—close to it, humbly opining. *Juvenescence.* The state or period of being young. As in the flickering of fireflies. Larry Rios, while at the newspaper, found unpreservable acquaintanceship with a half-Panamanian reporter who'd told him America was a blindfolded babe shepherded off a cliff. Faulkner was wrong, he said. History's not alive, it's a bloated corpse of malicious inaction. Raised without mothering, Larry felt for the guy. Marginally.

291. Flung

Once there was a writer who killed so many folks in his stories that he was granted permission to try it himself for real. He was old enough to know better, young enough to believe he'd do the right thing. An extraordinary experience burning a key player off the face of the map. Billowing smoke. Crackling fireball separating soul from body. Life's cheap. He co-produced his secondary character, happiness in mind, scourges notwithstanding in his own backyard. Tell yourself they're not real. What pleasures, flung into Davy Jones' locker (a furnace located in South Texas). Fight fire with fire—then what?

292. Notifies

San Antonio is devouring breakfast tacos while watching the Tower of the Americas prick the clouds. San Antonio is sullying white Tim Duncan jerseys with green salsa. San Antonio is recommending graphic novels to gregarious immigrants residing in the medical center. San Antonio is a brown pickup truck with a rear-window decal that says *Brown Sugar*. San Antonio is mariachi music meets Mozart dressed as Our Lady of Guadalupe. San Antonio is frog poems rendering the page soggy. As Larry Rios writes, Yuks the sword-swallowing frog finally notifies him, "I'm actually a girl, man." Larry, mortified, is thus freed. (For today.)

293. Muscle Memory

He locates in the back of his closet the denim jacket that belonged to his father, on the back of it the phrase *WAR IS HELL* embroidered in red. William Tecumseh Sherman—a poet for all seasons. He reaches inside the jacket's interior pocket, retrieves a small paper folded in four, the numbers on the note lost to permanent marker ink. So as not to be tempted. But then the phenomenon of muscle memory kicks in, her digits illumining themselves as though cascaded down from *The Matrix* servers, the Garden of Eden. Inhalation. Ring ring. Awaken, my beloved. Let us speak.

294. Propriety

What follows is a staid tête-à-tête between man and former wife—woman and former husband. Out of respect for the survivors who've suffered mightily, most of their discussion remains confidential. Private, as it must. But I'm not your Fly on the wall for nothing. No—I skirt to the bleeding edge of propriety and there I percolate. And report: "I only know you through having loved me," says he, "and nobody else. But tell me: there's another man, right?" "Right." "Your birthright, right?" "Right." "If I could go back—but the point is, we can go anywhere but back, right?" "Right."

295. Unforgiven

"What I can't forgive you for, what I can't unsee, is the knife and gun in your hands. You next to Comet. Looming over her. The knife and gun. I have nightmares about the look in your eyes. Do you understand what could've happened?" "Don't condescend me, Luz. I told you—I saw her beside Comet. Reaching. Trying to take her. I needed to do something. Needed to protect her. She already took everybody else. So I had to kill her. But she ended up killing me, see." She ended up calling everybody back, he doesn't say, verklempt, body suddenly chilled.

And then as though nuking the enormous elephant in the room—the gigantic circus behemoth between their airwaves steadily settling into its integument—she asks: "But why the fuck would you bring a knife and a gun to a fight with the Devil?" Seconds crawl by. Then he laughs loudly, unashamedly, painfully. Defeated. It's the most unanswerable inquiry he'll leave unanswered. So astute, he thinks. Even her silences are unresolvable questions. The unfairer halves stand not a chance. "What's so hilarious?" she asks. "Nothing," then, "Everything. Irreconcilable differences." "Larry," she says, breaking, "you're smoking. I can taste the tar from here."

297. Scrambling

"We're permitted so many dreams, each endless as imagination, and I searching for you, grasping—never touching—awakening to find one half here, hardly recognizable, growing older, the other there, under my eyelids, the Light unreachable as God." Their call ends on a word, spoken through tears: "Paz." Peace. Her voice? His? It's enough. He'll be here as long as he can cope, until he can't. "Little happy me," he says to his tatty Chucks down below—shoegazing—thumbs between beltloops. "Me little happy," the snappy scrambling doing the trick, as if he's a Martian who finally decodes Earth's lingua franca.

298. Chorus

Every life's a dream life. Every life: dreaming. Every life dreamt before slithering onto the scene. Larry Rios, stewing on it, knows without doubt that Professors Masterson and Dupré also saw The Snake-Haired Lady—someway, somehow. In some half-lit classroom, they're still lecturing, unaccountably spry, insatiable. Age-old sacrifices commissioned by the same sovereign, their idiosyncratic tutelage still pushing kids into poetry, certainly not for wealth, wellbeing. Experts in the dark recapitulating the same designs. This darkness, the revolution, inglorious melee—it doesn't really die. Not how you think. Hold on. Hang tight. The outrage of eons, expansion—a chorus. Never-ending screams.

299. Favorite Dream

An intimate venue in Texas. Someone's backyard. Dusk. Buddy Holly and Etta James, after a duet, slow dance onstage. Etta removes Buddy's glasses. "You make a guy feel like a million bucks," Buddy purrs in Etta's ear. The merrymakers. Spectators whistling and cheering. As Buddy and Etta hug, Etta wishes to never let him go. She does, knowing Buddy must board the Bonanza—go and succumb to ash. As Buddy struts away, he turns around, glint in his gaze, blows Etta a kiss, which she returns. Sooner than they think, they'll return as one. Unified. Complete. This: Larry Rios' favorite dream.

300a. Roads

Love and death're the only certainties. Roads, what're those? Everywhere disrepair and so the necessity to fly—or shovel. Words atop words. Obstacles through which he'll tunnel. On the other side, recycled bodies—some sympathizers, some archenemies—will welcome him, someway, once the fog burns. Larry's folks died before he turned twenty-five. The pain will keep keeping him alive. Will he use the help he finds? Find himself missing? Predestiny's trickery. The last male (not zero) of his line. Dark matter of time. Monstrous god-motor of motion from which creativity is an astronomical gift. Rising sun: our greatest sleight of hand.

She had a god complex and I was miserably in love. Start of a novel? Abandoning poetry already, Larry Rios? His head's in a paper bag. He's a charged point on the line. The line is all we have. And the shape between point A and point Z—everything, milove. Writing is the death of him. Death's the beginning. Anything is findable. Just search harder. Larry dies forever. Words as scorned flesh pulled back to a smile, torqued joy tearing the chains. Paralysis. Dilapidation. Conflagration. Rejuvenation. But why *miserably in love*? He doesn't know; he'll find out. One way; nohow. Amen.

300c. Worthy

Larry Rios, crying quietly, drives home from the children's hospital. Volunteering to read to terminally ill youth is the hardest thing he's done. Worthy of his fleeting vitality, time—not much left. Aaliyah—whose parents named her after the singer—who this year will fall to Ewing sarcoma, said to Larry earlier: Yuks is iconic—I wanna write frog poems just like you. She shared: You made today hurt less, friend. Larry asked: Can I come back? She answered: I'll be here, fam, convalescing. (Larry—keep making today hurt less. Living won't get easier, I'm afraid. But I promise we'll survive.)

I promise.

Bruce Lee

ACKNOWLEDGEMENTS

To Ito Romo, again, for opening the floodgates. To Mom and Pops, my brothers and sister and cousins, for grounding energy. To Robert Aaron Salinas, for reading the first draft in its sorriest glory. To John Irving, for *The World According to Garp*. To the ghost of Roberto Bolaño, for visiting. To the ghost of James Baldwin, for lending its likeness. To the music of John Coltrane and Caroline Rose, for assuaging the pain of thinking through a pandemic. To Richard Swift's "Broken Finger Blues," for pushing me past the finish line. To Cyra Dumitru, for showing me a thing or two about poetry. To Analicia Perez, for showing me a thing or two about poetry first. To Anndria Flores, for putting that sticky note on my cubicle. To my booksellers and baristas, for making a guy feel like a million bucks. To Edward Vidaurre, for extraordinary belief. To Avery Castillo, for handling business with grace. To Ursula Villarreal-Moura and Fernando A. Flores, for saying *hell yes*. To Lisa Oakes and Daniel Paniagua, for the magic of art. To Luis Cuahtémoc Berriozábal, for your poem, "Let Everyone In" (the inspiration for Chapter 280). And to Jennifer Lloyd, for being the best listener this side of the Alamo—again, again, again.

ABOUT THE AUTHOR

Alex Z. Salinas is the author of four volumes of poetry, most recently *Hispanic Sonnets* and *Trash Poems*. His book of stories, *City Lights From the Upside Down*, was included in the National Book Critics Circle's *Critical Notes*. He lives in South Texas. *The Dream Life of Larry Rios* is his first novel.

www.ingramcontent.com/pod-product-compliance
Lightning Source LLC
Chambersburg PA
CBHW021229310726
48971CB00006B/1746